# STRONG

Strong
Copyright © 2021 by Kyle Viera

Illustrations by Vladimir Shvachko

ISBN: 978-1-7355420-0-3

First Edition

Printed in USA by 48 Hour Books for Hidden Pen Pressings

# STRONG

Kyle Viera

-Hidden Pen Pressings-

*For Luke*

# I

The boy lay awake in the silent semidarkness, careful not to make a sound. The folding cot beneath him sagged on one side, but after countless nights he'd grown used to it. Rows of these beds filled the dim room, each occupied by another young man sound asleep under a patchwork blanket. With everyone else snoring, grumbling, drooling, the boy found himself the only waking soul in the room. For his sake, he hoped it stayed that way.

Dawn crept through the window above his head, past the bars caging the grimy glass. He kept still and quiet, moving only his thumbs to turn the pages of the book in his hands. The thing looked as old as printing itself, a stack of thick yellow sheets stitched into faded leather binding. Before flipping each page he gave a glance around, trying to remain quiet as possible. The last thing he wanted to do was wake anyone, not while the story was getting good.

He could picture the torch flickering in his hand as he sprinted down the black hall, his ironclad boots pounding the damp stone floor. Left, right, left again, he charged through the cavernous corridors, each darker than the last as he went further into the deep. Crouching kept his face out of the cobwebs clinging to the decaying stone ceiling. Behind a sheet of milky strands a skeleton was lashed against one wall, jawbone hanging in its final scream.

Drawing the sword at his hip he took another turn, guided into the darkness by some mysterious unseen force. The path grew narrower, rockier, his torch the only source of light. He was getting close now, he could feel it-

Mumbling came from the cot beside him and fear gripped him like a sharp claw. The book flew under his blanket, his heart pounding as he pretended to sleep. When the sound went still he cracked an eyelid and saw the kid had rolled over and continued to snore. He gave it a full minute before sliding the book back out and returning to the dungeon. If he was caught, if someone saw him... no, he couldn't bear to think of it.

At last there it was, a green light at the end of the hall, eclipsing an arched doorway some thirty yards ahead. As he dashed forward he heard a scratching, clicking sound moving fast across the ceiling in his direction. The torch revealed two massive spiders dropping from the webs, each pulsing hairy leg over three feet in length. With pincers raised one of them lunged, crossing the gap between them with a single spring.

The sword slashed and sick green sprayed the web covered walls. Legs thrashed and twitched on the rocky floor as a foul liquid poured from a gash in the spider's abdomen. He thrust the sword through its head as the other came skittering forward, bringing his blade up just in time to block the frantic fangs. His torch batted the arachnid aside with a flutter of flame, as more scuttling closed in above him.

A third spider landed right beside him, its cluster of eyes gleaming in the torchlight. He booted it down the hall as it went for his leg, into a sheet of its own glistening web. His weapon carved through the other as he cocked back and flung the torch at the last monster. It spun in a wheel of orange light and speared the struggling spider to the wall. Glowing webs dripped as the legs curled and kicked, a burning stench filling the already rank passageway.

He recovered his torch as he passed the singed spider, the end still hot and flickering. With sword raised and eyes on the ceiling he made his way toward the door. The light brightened as he approached, the dangling webs like a guard of green ghosts. Sheathing his blade as he stood before the smooth stone slab, he raised a hand and pressed his palm against it, an instant rush of energy shooting up his arm.

The door trembled and with a flash it vanished, the green light pouring over him. He squinted as he entered the small, circular room and found a pedestal at the center, a box studded in emerald resting on it. The light was seeping out from under its lid, radiating inviting warmth like the springtime sun. A tingle ran up his spine as he placed his hands on it, and slowly opened the lid-

A whistle screeched in the silent room and the book disappeared under the blanket once more. Cots creaked as the boys sprang from their beds, each of them dressed in the same striped nightshirt. They hurried into line in front of an old woman in a faded gray frock, a silver whistle protruding from her lips. She raised a crooked forefinger and counted them off, eyes narrowed behind her rimless spectacles.

The boy folded the corner of the page to mark his spot then slipped the book into a tear under his bed. As she counted the last of them the old woman noticed him still hunched over his crooked cot, her weathered face dropping into a frown. A sudden shadow cast over him as he turned to join the line, his nervous reflection looking back at him from a pair of dirty lenses.

"Sorry, Mistress Agatha, I was just making my bed."

"That's twice this week you've lined up late. One more time and I'll start waking you myself!"

She aimed a kick at the seat of his pants as he hurried to the end of the line. Her whistle puffed again and single file they went, into the drafty hallway and down a spiral staircase to a room lined with a row of cubbies. The boy dressed in his patched trousers and

3

wrinkled shirt, his toes an inch from the tips in his shoes. He pulled his worn cap over his short brown hair and put on his beat-up old coat, catching the tiny name written inside the collar as he swung it around his shoulders.

## *Sam*

He lined up as the last of them got into place, Agatha not batting an eye at any of those boys getting there late. They were led to a cold cafeteria with two long tables surrounded with stools and an overpowering smell of cheese. Another elderly woman stood by a cauldron-like pot with a heavy wooden spoon in her wrinkled hands. They waited their turn as she doled out scoops of sloppy porridge into bowls for each of them, the tables filling in minutes.

When Sam finally reached her he was still rubbing his backside where Agatha's pointed shoe had landed. The spoon scraped at the sides and bottom of the pot, leaving him with less than half of what the others had gotten. Sensing he wasn't happy about his portion, the woman gave a threatening jab of her spoon. "Line up sooner next time, you bloody ingrates are lucky you eat as well as you do. Now out of my sight before I report you to Agatha."

He took his bowl and turned away, chatter and the sound of scraping spoons filling the tables. Both were already packed, the boys sitting elbow to elbow as they ate. As he suspected there wasn't a single empty seat left for him. Some of the other kids watched as he walked back and forth, sniggering and whispering to one another behind their hands as he searched for a stool.

A dark haired young man at the table to his right waved him over, sliding a stool out from under the table across from him. Sam placed his bowl on the table and took a seat, and before he grabbed his spoon his seat was gone. Everyone burst with laughter as the stool crumpled beneath him, its legs rolling away in all directions. The dark haired boy and his friends roared with glee, practically falling off their stools themselves.

4

"I can't believe you fell for that!" The kid laughed. "I've been waiting for someone to sit on that thing all week!"

"Real funny," Sam muttered as he got up.

"It was just a joke," the other said. "Unless you want to make something of it?"

He and several of his friends stood up, threatening looks on each of their faces. Another sharp whistle blast made everyone jump and brought the room to silence. Sam grabbed his bowl and moved to a corner, sitting cross-legged on the floor with his breakfast. The crusty dregs of the porridge pot were especially dry today, and more than once he pulled a splinter of wooden spoon from between his lips.

Agatha's whistle went off again before most of them had finished their bowls. Another dull, dusty corridor brought them to a high-ceilinged atrium, the rounded walls flaking and free of decoration. The old woman stood watching them in front of a set of double doors, two slabs of rough, unfinished wood that stretched up almost twice her height.

"The Foundry sent a messenger this morning. Those of you scheduled today are to report to the warehouse at 8:00 sharp. The foreman reports all tardiness, so I will find out if anyone's been lollygagging. I've also been informed that extended shifts will be mandatory until further notice."

Half of the boys groaned, Sam included, but fell quiet under Agatha's stony gaze. She cleared her throat with a toadlike grumble, her eyes moving with contempt from face to face.

"The rest of you head back to the kitchens and help Beatrice clean the place up. When you're done with her you can take your weekly recess." Some of the boys gave hushed cheers in spite of the old woman's glare. "Don't forget that when you're about town you represent this institution, and by extension myself. Anyone caught out of line or who hasn't returned by 7:00 on the dot will have me to deal with."

Judging by their faces each of them knew too well what that meant. She swung open the doors onto the landing outside, flanked by two stone staircases leading down the left and right. More than half of them marched out the door and down the steps, somber as a funeral march. Agatha's whistle could already be heard screeching as she slammed the doors shut behind them.

It was a grey morning in the city of Farstone, the sun already losing its fight with the cold clouds overhead. Sam looked up at the building he'd just exited, as dismal on the outside as it was within. A square granite structure with windows hung with bars, the place looked more like a prison than it did a home for children. It was the only home Sam had ever known, but he felt as welcome there as the rodents and roaches crawling in its walls.

The streets were lively with conversation and the clatter of coach wheels on cobblestone. Men and women bustled up and down the sidewalks, heading to work or one of the many stores and businesses. Shopkeepers swept out their entrances or arranged wares in windows in preparation for the days' customers. Merchants pushing carts of goods squabbled at every corner over rights to where each could set up for the day.

Sam walked across Knot Street headed toward the Foundry, holding his coat closed against the wind. Winter hadn't arrived yet but it was well on its way, a biting chill in the noisy, horse-scented air. The closeness of the crowd provided some warmth as he pushed his way through the petticoats and hoopskirts. Voices all around him were haggling over quality and pricing while others shouted out their daily deals to reel in potential buyers.

He looked up at the city's clock tower and saw he had less than half an hour before his shift began. Knot Street Orphanage and Farstone Steel Company participated in what Agatha called a "sub-sidized labor program", which to Sam was a fancy way of saying he and the other kids worked their tails off for tattered clothes and a few cold scoops of porridge a day. Hardly a fair wage, but the boys were in no position to bargain; it was either that or trying to scrape a living out on the streets.

With each slow step the dread of his destination grew stronger. He was still exhausted from his double shift the day before, his hands were stiff and his back felt years older than it should. Local laws protected children from working excessive amounts of hours, but the Foundry was sure to hit the legal maximum every week. If given their way those greedy tyrants would have them working every waking moment in the sweltering mill.

It was so crowded this morning that there wasn't a single cobblestone without a shoe standing on it. Sam fought his way through to avoid suffocating as much as being late. At the corner of Crest and High Street he came within an inch of getting plowed by a horse-drawn carriage. The bearded coachman barked a slur at him as he lashed the leather reigns in his hands. In avoiding the carriage he backed into a man standing on the curb, who snarled like Sam had made some unforgivable insult.

"Watch it, street rat!"

The man shouldered past him and stomped across Crest Street, almost getting hit himself by another carriage. An old woman went next and bumped him with the basket hooked on her frail arm. Wherever Sam moved he ran the risk of being trampled, and with the slow lurch of the mob it was going to take him days to reach the Foundry. Luckily he knew another way, quick, direct, and traffic-free... if you had the stomach for it.

He slipped between two buildings and over to a sewer grate, a metal grid blocking a small dripping opening. He pulled it off and slipped inside before any monocle-ringed eyes nearby spotted him. The stink hung around him like fog as he replaced the grate, the sewer floor slick with dark slime. He started jogging east, guided by light slipping through the grates running along the streets.

The bustle of the townspeople could be heard overhead, their voices muffled by several feet of brick and dirt. Squeaking echoed off the rounded walls from the rats scurrying along the filthy floor. Most would have found using the underground network revolting, but Sam used it so often he felt almost at home down here. Almost.

He picked up a stick and gripped it with two hands like a sword in front of him. Aside from the smell he didn't imagine this place being much different from the dungeon in his book. He could picture the spiders scuttling at him, their hairy bodies throbbing as the pincers gave eager twitches. His battle cries echoed through the tunnel as he took down his pretend enemies, the stick making rapid swishes through the stinking air.

Continuing down the path he knew by heart, he reached the other side of town in no time at all. Not only did the sewers cut any trip around town in half, they served another purpose as well. Farstone's streets were plagued by gangs and ruffians, most of them kids not much older than Sam. Running into a group of them spelled disaster for a scrawny kid like him. It may have stunk to high heaven down here, but at least it was safe.

He tossed his weapon like the hero in the story had done with his torch as he reached the grate on Foundry Road. A nearby woman in thick furs saw him crawl out, turning her nose and walking at a smart pace up the street. Sam was amused at the effect he'd had on her as he kicked muck off his shoes and straightened his coat, standing in the shadow of the structure beside him.

Farstone Steel was the largest building in town, a red brick mesa crowned with three blackened smokestacks. Steam was trailing from each of them as the morning fires began to warm up. Sam walked toward the main entrance, where a line of workers were filing into the building. They ranged in age from old men to even younger than Sam, all of them in tattered, stained work clothes.

The line led up the brick staircase to a set of doors, where a stench of burning oil hit Sam's face like a fist. Inside there was a cacophony of clanking steel, cursing voices, and the grinding whirr of machinery. They walked down a wide brick corridor, the walls plastered with safety warnings and directions around the complex. Walking down this stretch always gave Sam a sense like he and the other workers were cattle being led to slaughter.

Like the Orphanage he had a cubby at the Foundry, where he found goggles, gloves, and his heavy leather apron. He rested the goggles on his head and followed a sign with a red arrow reading STEEL ROOM 3. The noise grew louder until it felt like his skull was shaking in its skin. One thing the Foundry didn't provide was hearing protection, as a headache didn't affect productivity in quite the way the loss of a finger or an eye did.

He followed the other workers into a massive room filled with all sorts of ironworking equipment. Molten steel poured from vats into molds that flashed and flared with orange light. Men pounded red-hot rods into shape with heavy hammers before quenching them in oil. A row of huge presses stamped hunks of hot metal in to different shapes, fabricating fittings and parts for just about everything imaginable. Bits of iron and sparks were flying everywhere, the oil-stained floor littered with steel scraps.

Sam found the foreman, a dark haired man with heavy eyebrows stuffed behind his goggles. They contracted at Sam's approach, the man pulling Sam's scratched lenses down over his face.

"Get those things on, dammit! You want to lose an eye before you even start?"

"Sorry, sir," Sam adjusted the goggles to where they belonged. "Where am I working today?"

"Chain," The man grunted. "Someone lost a thumb in the press earlier so they're a man short, and we have a big order going to the cove tomorrow. Well, what are you waiting for? Get to it!"

The surrounding noise hid Sam's curse from the foreman. He headed over to the chain department and was put at a press, where he spent his shift making more than a mile of hot, heavy links. His hands were cramping up in the oversized gloves as the

9

time inched agonizingly by. The older workers around him all bore the same deadpan, lifeless expression, the will or even the thought of doing anything better with their lives worn out ages ago.

After ten grueling hours the warehouse shut down and Sam headed back, his ears ringing long after the noise stopped. The streets were far less crowded in the evening hours, the lampposts' soft light guiding the workers home for a few hours' sleep before resuming their work the next morning. Other kids from the Orphanage ran past him, laughing and joking with one another as they hurried back before Agatha's curfew.

Over a dozen of them went by and none of them greeted him or invited him to join them, none of them noticed that he'd been there at all. There were sixty-six other boys who called Knot Street Orphanage home, and there wasn't a single one that Sam would call a friend. It might have bothered another kid, but not Sam, not one bit... not with the book waiting marked at one of his favorite parts.

Without the throngs of townsfolk the walk home was quick and quiet. Merchants were packing up their carts and clearing the streets while shop signs rotated from 'open' to 'closed' in their windows. Only the taverns remained active, and Sam recognized more than one Foundry worker lingering outside of each one he passed. A group of vagabonds were singing around a flaming barrel on Crest Street, passing a fast-emptying bottle between them.

A few blocks from the Orphanage he heard something move on the sidewalk behind him. He turned but saw only the vagrants swaying and singing on the corner, paying him no attention at all. With a shrug he went to continue home when a pair of grubby hands grabbed his coat and pulled him into a nearby alleyway.

"Well, well, well," A tall, skinny kid pushed him against the wall, his cruel grin missing several teeth. "Haven't seen you for a while! Been avoiding us, eh?"

Sam stood with his back against the brick, staring right back at the taller boy. Beside him stood a runt of a kid with a mean, pudgy face, their ragged clothes heavy with the stink of sweat and stale tobacco. Though they had him cornered Sam stood his ground, not showing either an ounce of fear.

"So, what have you got for us today, freak? Got any coin on you?"

"No," Sam's reply was firm, and also truthful. "Just leave me alone, Jake."

"No?" The tall kid looked down at his cohort. "We'll see about that, won't we, Ernie?"

"Yeah," The short kid's smile held fewer teeth than his friend's. "I'll bet we can shake a few pennies out of 'em!"

Sam made a break for it just as Jake swung at him. The fist missed as Sam ducked and rushed to escape the alley. Ernie jumped in front of him before he could get away and tried to pin him against the wall. Sam pushed him off before Jake could throw another shot, but not before catching two of Ernie's knobby knuckles near his right eye.

Blood welled on his cheek as Sam sprinted down the street, the two hoodlums close on his heels. His shoes skidded on the cobblestones as he turned up an alley before Jake's grubby fingers seized the collar of his coat. The bullies bumped into each other as they stopped short and sped down the alley after him. They moved fast but Sam was already gone, leaving them chasing only the rats chirping on the ground.

The two swore and continued their hunt, not knowing they'd just been right on top of him. Sam had gotten the grate back into place moments before the flapping sole of Jake's shoe landed on it. With no light to guide him Sam stumbled his way back towards Knot Street, cringing at the dull throbbing in his eye. Emerging from a grate at the back of the Orphanage, Sam found Agatha waiting at the entrance, her trusty switch at the ready.

She noticed his face and her weapon hand lowered to her side. "What in blazes happened this time?"

"I got jumped again," Sam focused on the old woman with his good eye.

"Guess I won't need to handle it, then," Agatha almost sounded disappointed. "Well, get inside and clean yourself up. You've missed dinner, so straight up to bed when you're done."

Sam went to the washroom and cleaned off his face, dabbing his eye with a damp cloth. It had stopped bleeding but was bruised and sore, a thin blue slit peeking through the swelling. It could have been worse, he supposed. If he didn't know the sewers as well as he did he would've ended up with much worse than just a shiner.

When he got up to the cot room the rest of the boys were already taking to their beds. Some of them snickered as he walked past, pointing at him behind his back. Sam's cot shivered as he crawled into it, the torn side sagging inches lower than the other. He could feel a corner of the book poking him as he tried to make himself comfortable and covered up with his blanket.

Agatha extinguished the oil lamps as the last of the boys got into their cots. She stopped in the doorway and turned to them, her long, lumpy shadow cutting the room in two. "If I hear a single sound in here, I'll be right back in with my switch."

Threats like that were closest thing to a 'goodnight' the boys ever got. Cots creaked as everyone settled in, yawning and grumbling as the relief of sleep took them. One or two of them could already be heard snoring as the room at last went still. Sam was tired from work and his face ached something awful, but he wasn't ready for bed just yet. Once he was sure everyone had passed out he slipped out the book and flipped to where he'd left off.

The moon was bright enough to read without having to squint as the dungeon reappeared in his mind. His hands rested on the warm, glowing chest, the green glinting on his armor, when he heard the scratching speeding up the passageway behind him. With a grin and a flick of a page Sam charged, keeping a sharp eye on the door between each sword stroke. If given the choice at the moment, he'd rather see a dozen giant spiders come crawling at him than Agatha or Beatrice.

# II

When he woke the next morning, a horrifying sight made Sam nearly leap out of his cot. Resting open on his chest was the book, out in clear view for anyone to see. The pages had taken him well into the night, and he must've dozed off while reading. He had to be more careful than that. If Agatha or one of the other kids had noticed it sitting there it would have been disastrous.

He looked around the quiet, shadowed room and saw everyone still out cold. Overcast greeted him outside his barred window but it was enough to see, and he went right back to the story. As tired as he often was from working the Foundry he'd trained himself to get up an hour or so before everyone else to sneak in some adventure. This was his time, away from bullies and noisy machinery, lost between the worn leather covers.

Before long, though, the whistle burst at the door and the book went away without anyone seeing. Today Sam ended up well in the middle of the line to keep Agatha off his back. After he dressed he stopped at a grimy mirror and examined his face. He'd healed up well, quite well, in fact. The swollen eye was bright and blue as the other, the bloody cut all but vanished. Aside from a few freckles his face was as clear as any of the ones around him.

A few hours before he looked like he'd lost a boxing match, but now there wasn't a scratch on him. It would have shocked him, if it hadn't happened a hundred times before. Why this was he could never explain, nor could the Orphanage's nurses for that matter. Agatha often joked that she'd sell him to the circus if one ever came to town, or at least he hoped she'd been joking.

Down in the cafeteria the same cold blob of porridge as the day before waited for him. There was more in his bowl than yesterday, but still noticeably less than the kids before him. He should've known better than to make a face in front of Beatrice. He also noticed that everyone had a stool to sit on today, none of which broke apart. Hiding stools was just one of the many ways the kids at the Orphanage got their kicks at his expense.

After they ate he and the others lined up in the atrium, Agatha's resentful stare bearing down on them. Today was Sam's day off from the Foundry, but he'd still have to spend the better half of it washing pots or scrubbing floors, whatever unpleasant task the old crone threw his way. Still, any work around the Orphanage was easier than ten hours of laboring in the screeching, sweltering warehouse. Easier, and safer.

"The Foundry sent a messenger this morning," The old woman said. "The extended shifts have put them well over the legal hourly maximum you all are allowed to work for the week. As such, they've been forced to cut today's shifts."

Half of the boys cheered in celebration. Sam couldn't remember the last time shifts were cancelled; why couldn't this have happened on his day to work? Agatha piped on the whistle and the excitement ceased at once.

"Seeing as we have so many extra hands here today, we shall give this pigsty a thorough cleaning." Her crooked finger counted off half the crowd, Sam included. "You all head down to the kitchens, Beatrice needs all of the rat traps checked, and changed if need be. The rest of you follow me, there are about a hundred crates I need pulled from the attic, and I'm sure as hell not climbing up and down that rickety ladder."

Half the boys followed Agatha while the rest headed for the kitchens, but Sam didn't join them. Instead he slipped back to the stairway, careful not to be seen. Once he finished in the kitchens he thought he'd spend the rest of the day reading by the forest at the edge of town. He heard talk that wolves had been spotted in the woods recently, but he'd snuck out there several times in the past few weeks and hadn't seen as much as a pawprint.

The cot room was eerie when empty, the rows of folding beds lying unmade and abandoned. He took slow steps between them so his shoes wouldn't clack against the worn wooden floor. As he reached his own he thought he heard something move near the door, but saw nothing but empty cots. His hand plunged into the torn seam and pulled out the book, his fingers giving the cover an affectionate squeeze.

He was trying to tuck it into his coat when something in the doorway tripped him up. Laughter rang up the hall from two boys crouched on either side of him, the end of a string in each of their hands. The book flew from Sam's grip as he fell and slid across the floor. He clamored after it on all fours but one of the boys swiped it up before he could reach it, taunting him with cruel glee.

"Hey!" Sam tried to grab the book as it dangled above him. "Give it back!"

The boy tossed it to his friend with a whoop, who caught it and waved it over his head. "Come and get it, freak!"

Sam ran at him and he lobbed the book back to his fellow, whose face was turning red with laughter. Pages rustled as the book flapped back and forth through the air like a wounded bird. Sam's arms flailed over his head as he tried to grab it but the boys aimed it high above his reach.

"What's going on out here?"

All three of them spun around as the commanding voice cut through the cackling. A young woman stood in a doorway across the hall, dressed in the same drab frock as Agatha. Dark curls framed her face, her brown eyes on them in harsh scrutiny.

"Sorry, Miss Sarah," one of the boys said, all amusement gone from his voice. "Timmy and I were trying to stop this... this thief!"

"Y-yeah," His friend held up the book and pointed at Sam. "We... we caught him stealing this! We were just going to find someone, yeah, thank goodness you're here!"

She held out her hand and the boy snapped forward to present his find. She looked the book over then turned back to the two of them. "Thank you for bringing this to my attention. You two run along now, I'll deal with this."

Both shot Sam evil smirks and disappeared down the hall. The young woman nodded Sam through the door she stood in and closed it behind them. He looked up at her, his eyes doing a tentative dance between the book and the woman's gaze. She had the look of a young person who'd aged early under the weight of a stressful life, the slight lines forming by her eyes out of place on someone in the first half of their twenties.

"Not working the Foundry today?" she asked.

"No, Miss Sarah," Sam watched the book as he spoke. "Agatha said shifts were cancelled today."

"That's unusual," She noticed him watching the book and started flipping absently through the pages. "Doing a little light reading, were you?"

"A bit," he said, transfixed on his precious possession in her hands. The young woman gave him a thoughtful look, then smiled and handed the book to him. Sam returned her grin as he took it and looked it over for any damage. The cover was still intact and the pages still held tight by their stitching, nothing he could spot outside of the usual wear.

"Thanks, Miss Sarah. I thought those two jerks were going to ruin it tossing it like that."

"Anytime," she replied. "You ought to be more careful, though. If it had been Agatha instead of me all three of you would have been in for it."

"If it were anyone else, really," Sam added.

The entire room was coated in dust, down to the curls of faded green paper separating from the walls. A desk sat buried under piles of paperwork with several musty paintings propped against it. Old cots more broken down than even his were stacked in a corner beside a pile of soiled linen. Specks of dust hung in the slivers of sunlight from the room's solitary window, a cobwebbed archway concealed behind a stack of wooden crates.

"I've never been in here before," Sam said. "What is all this stuff?"

"A heap of useless junk if you ask me," Sarah began stuffing the old linen into a sack. "Half the rooms in this place are loaded with garbage Agatha's saved over the years. She stumbled across this one early this morning and graciously gave me the task of sorting it out." She gave a sour grin as she picked through the spotted old cloth. "Aren't I lucky?"

"You and me both, I'm off to the kitchens to help Beatrice. I think she hates me even more than Agatha does."

A cloud of dust puffed out from beneath the sheets into Sarah's face. Her button nose crumpled and she let out a sneeze, sending a spray of dust through the musty air. She shook her head as she pulled a handkerchief from her frock and wiped her weary face. Dust settled in her hair, making her look even farther beyond her years.

"Looks like you could use a hand," Sam said.

"Hmm," Sarah looked unsure. "Beatrice will notice you missing, won't she?"

Sam waved a carefree hand. "Shifts were cancelled, remember? She's got plenty of help. Besides, I think she'd be glad to be rid of me, anyway."

The two set to work, Sam stacking the paper littering the desk into neat piles while Sarah sorted through the rest of the linen on the floor. The dates on some of the papers were decades old, records of past kids unfortunate enough to call Knot Street home. Sam wondered if a record like this existed of him somewhere... if it did he could only imagine what Agatha might have written on it.

"I'm glad to see you looking well this morning," Sarah said as she continued to stuff the mountain of mildewed linen into the sack. "Agatha said you looked a little worse for wear when you got back from the Foundry last night."

"I bet she couldn't wait to tell someone," Sam remarked.

"Who was it this time?"

"Jake and Ernie," Sam tried not to breathe in too much dust as he shuffled sheets of paper.

Sarah shook her head. "They always were trouble, those two. I remember my first year here they started a fire in one of the broom closets. If I hadn't been nearby with a bucket of mop water handy the whole place might've burned down."

"Worthless creeps," Sam muttered, ruffling the paper in anger as the night before replayed in his head. "Ernie got me good this time, too, caught me right in the eye."

"You'd never know, by the look of you," She noted his unblemished face. "I see that gift of yours has helped you again."

"No one else thinks it's a gift. Everyone here thinks I'm a freak."

Sarah's shoulders slumped at the boy's words. She noticed his book sitting on a clean corner of the desk and pointed to it.

"How many times have you read that now?"

"Not sure, lost count somewhere around sixty."

Sarah smiled. "Hardly the sort of thing a freak could do, I'd say. I doubt any other boy here could read even a single page of that. I would know, I see them sleeping on their desks during my lessons."

With the desk organized the room looked much cleaner, and now that the linen was confined to the sack the smell of mildew had faded. Sarah pulled one of the crates from the windowsill and placed it on the now cleared desk. Sunlight poured in like a break in a dam as she rummaged through it, tossing odds and ends into another lumpy sack.

"We're doing pretty well," Sam said as he rolled the sack of linen to the other side of the room to better stop the smell. "Between the two of us we'll have this place clean in no time."

"Until the next one," Sarah sighed. "For every room I sort out Agatha fills two more with junk. She also decided to cancel the rest of my lessons for the week to keep cleaning. I must say that when I took the teaching position here, I wasn't told I'd be doubling as a housekeeper."

"You deserve better than this place," Sam said. "You should be teaching at the Academy uptown, you're smarter than anyone there. Not that I want you to leave," he tacked on quick, not wanting to sound ungrateful or rude.

"Well, thank you," Sarah said. "The dean did extend me a tempting offer after I'd graduated, but I chose to come here instead. Anyone attending the Academy has enough privilege in their lives. I wanted to give less fortunate kids a chance at an education and to make something of themselves." She tossed a bent candlestick into the sack. "These days, though, it seems I'm more Agatha's maid than an educator."

She grabbed the next box and looked through it with far less study than the first. She threw most of the stuff into the sack without giving it more than a momentary glance. Light flooded the room as more of the window was revealed, dust twinkling all around them like tiny daytime stars. Sam noticed that it was one of the few windows at the Orphanage not surrounded with bars.

Sarah gasped as a mouse popped over one of the corners and flew across the floor, into a crevice between two warped pieces of molding. She grabbed the last crate from the windowsill, and without looking dumped the entire thing right into the sack. Sam giggled as she dropped the empty box to the floor and shrugged. "It's been sitting here for decades and we've all gotten along just fine without whatever was in there, haven't we?"

"I think it's always worth a look," Sam said. "You've found some pretty good things sifting through this stuff. I got fifty cents selling that pewter teapot you found a few weeks back, remember? Jake and Ernie robbed it off me, but still..."

"True enough," Sarah admitted. "I guess it's not all garbage."

"And let's not forget this," The boy cradled the book in his hands as if it were bound it gold. "This I wouldn't trade for all the money in the Farstone Treasury."

"That was quite the find, wasn't it?" Sarah agreed. "It certainly is nice having someone around who appreciates books as much as I do."

"Just this one," Sam said. "Where'd you find it, anyway, another one of these junk rooms?"

"That? No, that I found in Agatha's study."

Sam blinked and Sarah smirked. "She'd cancelled my lesson to have me clean out her study, and if you think this room is bad, you ought to see hers. I found it in the back of a cupboard with a note in her handwriting that said 'found with child upon arrival'. When I saw the name inside, I knew right away who it belonged to. It went in a dustbin while I finished my work, and I smuggled it out with the trash."

"And she never asked about it?" Sam was now looking at the book as if it were some piece of illegal contraband.

"Never," she said with a wink.

A sudden glare came to Sam's eye as he looked at the worn leather cover. "She was probably never going to give it to me, that miserable old bat."

"I doubt she remembered she had it," Sarah did her best to sound neutral. "Even after she dug through what I threw out and salvaged what she thought was worth saving she never so much as mentioned it."

"Well it's mine now, thanks to you," Sam gave her a hug and she laughed in surprise. "If it weren't for you I never would've even known about it. It's as much a gift from you as it is my parents."

Sarah bit back the emotion welling in her chest. "Just be sure that Agatha never sees it, or it'll find its way into the trash for good." She eyed the book with interest. "Now, what was it called again? The Tales of the Strange?"

"Not the Strange, I've told you a hundred times! It's the Tales of the Strong!"

"Oh, the Strong, right," she said, tapping her forehead. "Refresh my memory, won't you?"

Sam opened the book and showed her some of the brilliant illustrations. "The Strong were the mightiest, most powerful warriors who ever lived. They lived in kingdoms hidden all over the world, in deep jungles or high in the mountains... some of them even lived in volcanoes, and in the glaciers way up north!"

"Heavens," Sarah said. "Neither of those would've been my first choice."

"None of that would've bothered the Strong," Sam said. "They had power me and you could only dream of!"

"That's 'you and I', remember our grammar lessons?" Sarah waved a playful finger at him. "Tell me again, what sort of powers did they have?"

"Well for starters, the Strong could lift huge loads of weight," He turned to a drawing of a woman freeing a man pinned under a massive boulder. "Even a young kid could lift half a ton!"

"I might've guessed that by their name," Sarah giggled. "I'll bet the Foundry would love to have a few Strong on their payroll!"

"That's not all," Sam flicked to a page with a drawing of a man fighting off a snarling bear, the beast held at bay by flames coming from the man's fingertips. "Each kingdom had its own unique power that set them apart. Some could control fire, or ice, some of them could even transform! There's a great story in here about a guy who could turn into an eagle, let me see here..."

"They sound like great heroes," Sarah replied as she watched him flip excitedly through the pages. "Young men need good role models like that to look up to these days."

"They weren't all good," Sam said. "The Strong had their fair share of villains, too." He showed her an illustration of a skeleton bursting from the dirt. "There were some that were so evil they had the power to raise the dead from their graves."

"Maybe you've been reading a bit too much," Sarah joked. "If I didn't know better, I'd say you think these Strong were real!"

Sam gave her a hopeful look. "Well, it could've been real, couldn't it? I mean, ages ago, far away... maybe?"

"You do have quite the imagination on you. You ought to think about writing a storybook of your own one day!"

"Good one, Miss Sarah. No one would be interested in a story about me, unless you want to hear about the adventures of Sam and the Sewer Rats."

Sarah brushed the cobwebs from the lock on the window and pushed the two panes open. The hinges creaked as their stiff joints moved for the first time in what must have been forever. Cool autumn air wafted in, recycling the staleness of the long-sealed room. Farstone stretched out in a field of brick and shingles, the Foundry's smokestacks pluming above it all.

"I know things have been hard for you here," Sarah said, "Harder than most that come through this place have it, but don't let any of that discourage you. You're the brightest boy I've ever met, and you have a great heart in spite of all you've been through.

No one can say what life has in store for us, but it's certain you'll have a far better story to tell than Jake and Ernie ever will."

That much was true, Sam thought to himself. A low bar indeed, but he supposed he'd have to take it for now. He stuffed the book in his jacket then turned from the window to Sarah. "I'll be sure to come back to tell you all about it. If you're still here, that is."

"For better or worse, I'm sure I will," Sarah said, sounding both tired and determined. "Someone has to keep you kids safe from-"

A sharp click came from behind them as the door swung open. Though the book was hidden Sam's arm shifted over his coat to ensure its outline wasn't visible.

"Mistress Agatha," Sarah gave the headmistress a nervous curtsey. The old woman ignored her, glaring at Sam with contempt. "I thought I sent you to the kitchens?"

"If I may, Mistress," Sarah whisked to his aid. "I saw young Sam passing and asked him to help me. He's done an excellent job so far-"

Agatha looked less than impressed. "Are you not capable of handling such a simple task yourself? I have no need of an inefficient assistant, Sandra."

Sam saw Sarah's eyes darken but she maintained her composure. "Of course, Mistress, I am more than capable." The young woman adopted a stern expression with Sam, the same one she'd given the two boys tossing his book. "Do as the Mistress says. Run along to the kitchens at once."

"Not so fast," Agatha pointed at him. "The Foundry just sent word there's been another accident, and they're a man down in the smelting department. Get yourself down there straightaway."

"I thought shifts were cancelled," Sam protested. "They hit their limit on hours, didn't they?"

"Don't worry," Agatha smiled. "You'll be working off the books."

24

"But it's not even my day to work-"

"You'll get down there with or without switch marks on your backside, the choice is yours."

He looked at Sarah but knew there was nothing she could do. With a defeated sigh Sam slumped from the room toward the stairs. Agatha called out to him as he trudged down the steps. "And be back by curfew, or you'll be sorry!"

She turned back to Sarah once the boy had gone. "Ingrate. All of them, bloody ingrates. Can't wait to turn that one loose."

"Sam is a good boy," Sarah said with the faintest hint of defiance. "I think he'll do great things when he leaves here."

The old woman laughed. "Get back to work."

Sarah heaved the sack into a corner and began arranging books on a nearby shelf. Agatha continued chuckling to herself as she slumped like a slug from the room. "Fifty-five years I've run this place, and not a one of these brats became much more than a petty ironworker. He'll grow up to be nothing, just like all the rest!"

# III

By the time the tarnished whistle above his head finally blared Sam was beyond exhausted. Every worker dropped their tasks the moment it screeched and trudged toward temporary freedom. Sam removed his goggles and pulled off his smoking gloves, flexing his fatigued fingers. Taking stiff steps, he fell into line with the rest of the workers and exited the main warehouse, grabbing the book from his cubby as he left.

Outside cold wind stung his face, the evening sky already growing dark. He turned west down High Street, beginning the long, tiresome walk back to the Orphanage. His body was aching all over, his head pounding from the endless racket of machinery. There would be no reading by the forest today, and even worse he still had his regularly scheduled shift in the morning. All he wanted was to get back to the Orphanage and collapse into his cot.

Most of the town was preparing to turn in for the night. Some of the shopkeepers were already lighting the streetlamps outside their businesses. They shot Sam dubious looks as he passed, retreating inside their establishments and locking their doors with audible clicks. Sam didn't care. He had as little use for them as they did him. As far as he was concerned, he had everything he needed tucked safely in his coat.

Still, there were times when his loneliness did get to him, and today was one such day. He wondered what it would be like to have a family... he pictured some anonymous mother busy with dinner, a faceless father whittling by an imaginary fireplace while whatever siblings he might have had squabbled on the floor at the man's knee. His fingers traced the edge of the book as the idea passed him by like a dream within a dream.

At the corner of West Crossing the clock tower struck half past the hour. His surprise shift went longer than he realized, and he needed to move fast to get back on time. It was too dark to use the sewers, so cutting through the back alleys was his only option. There was the risk of running into the likes of Jake and Ernie, but he'd already gotten on Agatha's bad side once today. He waited for a carriage to pass then slipped between two brick buildings, his fingers crossed in his oversized sleeve.

Rats squealed as he jogged down the dark brick corridor, light from the streets reaching him in spotty bursts. His knowledge of Farstone's backways rivaled that of the sewers, and he made it to the other side of town in less than twenty minutes. To his relief the alleys were mostly deserted, no sleeping vagrants or singing drunkards, and best of all, no Jake or Ernie.

As he continued through the maze of red brick and cobblestone his thoughts lingered on his family. There were many nights when he lay awake in his cot, not reading but wondering, who they were, why they left him on the Orphanage steps, with a storybook of all things. Maybe they thought he'd enjoy it, or perhaps it was the only possession they had to their name. They must have cared a little, or they wouldn't have left anything at all, would they?

The book itself gave him no leads. He'd searched every page for an author's name or publisher seal, some clue of where it came from, but found no markings outside of the title and his name penned on the inside cover. It was obvious the thing was old, so it may have even been bound by hand. That probably explained why it held up so well against the untold years, and the occasional surprise game of keep-away.

In the end, he was left only to guess. He was on his own and that was the way things were, stuck at a wayward orphanage working a backbreaking job, with no idea how or why he got there. Not for long, though. Within a year the Orphanage would turn him loose and he'd be off on his own adventure, just like the Strong in his book. Granted he wouldn't be lifting boulders or conjuring fire, but it had to be better than what the sewers had to offer.

He got a whiff of sewer between Stone & Stone Tailors and Martin's Alehouse, and noticed an open grate on the ground. Glass crunched under his shoes as he avoided the dark, dank opening, and he saw a broken window gaping on the deserted tavern. Empty barrels were stacked against the wall along with one filled with rubbish. His peaceful yet lonely walk was suddenly ended, as a screech in the dark made him jump almost to the tavern roof.

A cat pounced from a high barrel, its claws stretched out at him. Sam leaned back to avoid his scruffy attacker and fell to the ground. It hissed as it landed then stalked off, its filthy fur standing on end. Even the mangy beasts of Farstone's streets couldn't seem to give him a break. He went to leave when the barrels wobbled and a shadow appeared from behind them, blocking the way.

"Flea-bitten old...Well, what have we here?"

Sam recognized the voice, he knew it only too well. A tall boy in his late teens emerged from behind the barrels, the bottom of his gut hanging out under his dirty, undersized shirt. His curly blonde hair was as grimy as his fat, sweaty face, a half-drained bottle of amber liquid in his pudgy hand.

"Big Len," Sam breathed.

"That's me," The two words came out in a single sound. The stench of stale liquor filled Sam's nostrils as the massive kid got closer, a cock-eyed grin on his boyish face. "Missed me, did you?"

Sam had never missed anyone less. "I thought they locked you up in the juvenile detention center."

"They let me off early," The big kid took another step closer, swinging the bottle with his words. "Good behavior, see. I was a model inmate, I was!" Sam took a step back as Len staggered, almost knocking the stack of barrels onto him. "Hey, don't look so glum, you're just in time for the celebration!"

Sam had dealt with Big Len plenty of times before: strong as a bull but slow as could be, and given how little was left in that bottle the oaf likely wouldn't make it more than a few steps before falling on his flabby face. If Sam moved fast he could make it back to the Orphanage in one piece, and quite possibly on time.

Without another word Sam bolted up the alley, but saw none other than Jake and Ernie crawling from the broken window finishing bottles of their own. He slid to a stop as they blocked his only exit, laughing as they let their empty bottles crash on the ground.

"Well look who it is," Ernie slurred, his beady bloodshot eyes on Sam. "What's your scrawny hide doing on our turf?"

"Your turf?" Sam said, surprised at his own defiance. He knew what a serious spot he was in, but something inside stopped him from backing down. "Since when?"

"Let's see..." Big Len took a long drink, dribbling booze down his straining shirt. "Since right now, I'm thinking."

Jake and Ernie gave oafish giggles as they stepped up right behind Sam. The burn of alcohol made his eyes water as they pushed him towards their leader. Len stumbled closer, waving the bottle as he spoke. "Now I'll ask one more time, what the hell is a stinking orphan rat like you doing in my alley?"

"I'm just trying to get home."

The big boy laughed, his gut shaking as he took another swig. "You hear that, boys? Trying to get home! People have to want you there to make it a home. No one cares if you're dead or alive, any of you bloody orphans! You should all be sent down to the sewers where you belong, with all the other rats!"

Sam was holding his ground, his blue eyes locked with the bleary red ones above him. "Just leave me alone, I don't want any trouble."

"And what if we do?" Jake said.

A skinny hand pushed him from behind and Sam hit the ground in an instant. The book flew from his jacket, skidding along the cobblestones and stopping in front of Big Len's buckled shoes. Sam tried to grab it but a foot each from Jake and Ernie pinned him down. Len stooped and picked it up, nearly tipping forward as his body struggled to bend.

"What is it?" Ernie asked as Len straightened up, examining the book upside down.

"A book," Sam said, again unable to stop himself. "Ever heard of one?"

"Think you're funny, do you?" the little brute said. "Think you're real smart, eh? How's *this* for smart?"

He gave Sam a kick in the ribs, knocking his wind out. They yanked him to his feet as he gasped and coughed, doubled over as he tried to regain his breath. Len flipped through the book, drops of liquor staining the pages.

"Books, who needs 'em? Never read anything before in my life, and look at me, Big Len runs these streets! See where reading books gets you, orphan rat? Don't you worry, though, I'll get rid of it for you."

"No!"

Sam struggled to free himself as Len dropped the book into the barrel of trash and poured the remainder of the liquor over it. He pulled a matchbox from his pocket, struck one behind his ear, and let it drop. Hot tears ran down Sam's face as a fire burst in the barrel, the alley filled with light and the bullies' cruel laughter.

"What a baby," Jake sneered. "Did Mummy leave that for you?"

Ernie cackled then turned to Big Len. "Can we rough him up now, boss?"

"Doesn't matter if we do, though, does it?" The oafish boy glared at Sam through his glazed eyes. "I remember this kid, I've pounded him a hundred times, beat him all you want and the next day not a bruise on him! Even broke his nose once, and by morning there was nothing! It ain't natural, I tell you, he's a freak, that's what he is, a bloody freak!"

Sam didn't hear him. He was no longer struggling. He stared into the flames as they swallowed his treasure, his escape, the only piece of his family he'd ever known. His teeth gritted as Big Len raised his bottle and broke the bottom against the alehouse wall. He stumbled towards Sam, his evil grin illuminated in the firelight, pointing the jagged glass.

"Bring 'em over here, boys... Let's see if this does the trick."

He lunged and thrust the bottle into Sam's abdomen. The glass was about to bite when Sam's left arm broke free of Jake's grip and seized Len's greasy hand. The big boy cried as his sausage-like fingers crunched in Sam's, shards of glass forced deep into his palm. He dropped to the ground and cradled his crumpled hand, howling incoherent curses to the night.

Without thinking, without looking, Sam made a fist with his free hand and sent it at Ernie. He felt the few remaining teeth cave against his knuckles as blood sprayed from the tobacco stained lips. With his captors off him Sam kicked Ernie's stubby legs, dropping him to the cobblestones before even Sam realized what was happening. Ernie covered his mouth with his grubby hands as his gargled groans mingled with his superior's.

Jake swore and made mad, drunken swings for Sam's head. Instinct and common sense told him to just run for it, but instead Sam watched his own skinny forearm swing forward to block the

31

next blow. There was a sickening crack as Jake's arm snapped like a dried branch against his. Before the bully could scream Sam seized the shattered limb and flipped him, clear over his head, and slammed him onto Len's wailing form.

Sam stood panting, staring down in disbelief at the three groaning masses. Big Len's eyes were wide with fear as they darted from Sam to his battered comrades, his hand wrapped in his shirt.

"D-don't come any closer!" he whimpered, his voice cracking as he shuffled away. "Bloody f-freak!"

Sam watched as he and his lackeys hobbled out of the alley as fast as their battered bodies would take them, their moaning still audible after they vanished. Darkness returned as the last of the booze burned off, the rim of the barrel black and smoking. Tears still trailed down his face as he walked towards it, hoping some small part of it survived, a piece of the cover or a toasted page, anything he could still keep close...

The barrel's contents were nothing now but ash and soot. Sam brushed the debris aside and saw the cover of the book still sitting in the center. Forgetting any concern for burning himself he reached in and picked it up, but saw it was stuck in place. He grabbed with both hands and managed to pull it loose, and found the rest of the book still dangling from it.

Incredulous, he turned it in his hands and examined it. The cover and spine were blackened with soot, but no part of the book had ignited. He flipped through the pages and found them dry and crisp as they had ever been, each one tight in its place. Sam couldn't believe his eyes. The blaze should have incinerated the thing like kindling but here it was, worn as ever but still completely intact.

"What the-"

From somewhere far above him the clock tower's bells rang out the hour. He stowed the dirty book in his jacket and headed out of the alley towards Knot Street. He'd only taken a few steps when he heard movement behind him, a flapping sound like rustling fabric. Still heady from his fight, he turned and held his arms out in as threatening a way as he could muster.

"You want some more?"

It wasn't Big Len, or Jake or Ernie. A lone figure stood at the opposite end of the alley, hidden beneath a black cloak.

"That was impressive," the stranger said in a rasping, rattling hiss.

"Uh, thanks," Sam replied. The fight must've awoken a nearby vagabond the shadows had hidden from view. Sam turned to leave when the man took a step forward, pointing a thin hand at him. "What is your name, young man?"

Sam didn't answer and kept moving. He had no coin to spare and was even shorter on time. The man gave a laugh, a deep, throaty wheeze, then reached up and removed his hood. His skin was a pale, ghostly grey, stretched tight across his sunken face. He had grizzled white hair slicked back from his high forehead, stubble lining his pointed chin. If not for the fact that he was standing and speaking, Sam would have thought he was a corpse.

"They call me Bones, the pleasure is all mine." With the hood lowered Sam could see the glint of armor under the man's cloak. He took a step forward and Sam took one back, the stranger's smile widening. "This is a surprise indeed. Never in my wildest imagination did I expect to meet someone like you in this place. Tell me, how does such a small boy get to be so...*strong?*"

Somewhere in the distance Sam heard a shrill, piercing shriek, an unnatural sound unlike any bird or beast he'd ever heard. The man grinned as Sam continued to back away. "What is your hurry? We were just getting to be friends."

"Sorry, I really need to get going-"

"I don't think so," The man's eyes flashed as his voice went icy. "You are coming with me."

The ghoulish man stalked toward him, the temperature dropping with each echoing step. Sam turned to run but stopped dead in his tracks, as his legs became frozen in place. The man laughed as Sam struggled to move, but for some reason his whole body wouldn't budge. He was rooted on the spot, his escape only yards ahead of him, stuck like he was encased in some invisible concrete mixture.

Sam heard another screech and his body was suddenly free again. He turned and saw the man wrestling with a furry mass on his shoulder, the cat that jumped at Sam minutes before. The scrawny creature clawed and scratched as the man's shouts filled the alley. Sam pushed a stack of barrels and they toppled between the two buildings, separating himself and the struggling man.

He sprinted up the alley as fast as he could towards Knot Street. There was screaming and cries growing from the streets, along with a screeching wail that was certainly not coming from the cat. He was almost at the street when the ground disappeared beneath him, dropping him into darkness and the unmistakable stench of sewer.

# IV

The slick, twisting pipe came to an abrupt end and dumped Sam onto the slimy sewer floor. He got to his feet and took off running, unsure if he was being followed and unwilling to wait and find out. He couldn't see more than a few feet in front of him, but his knowledge of the underground network kept him from running headlong into any walls. With his hands out to guide him he turned right at a fork, a cadre of rats following at his heels.

Above he could hear shouting from the streets, muffled voices mingled with more of that strange shrieking he'd heard in the alley. He quickened his race through the dark, stumbling on the uneven floor. At the end he found a wall drain with a section of its grate hacked away and forced his way through the opening. It had been years since he'd crawled through here, and the pipe was a much tighter fit than he remembered.

At long last he reached the drain's mouth, a hole in the hills of the nearby forest. He caught his breath on the cold forest air, a refreshing change from the stink of the sewer. In his desperation to get away he'd gone as far as the sewer could take him. He was more than half a mile from town now, and there was still the dash back to the Orphanage... Agatha was going to have his head.

He started to jog as night crept in, his shoes squishing, his mind reeling. The book being unharmed by the fire was bizarre, but there must've been some logical explanation for that. What he did not have a logical explanation for was how in the world he managed to take on Big Len and his two cronies. How was he able to crush Len's hand like that, or throw Jake through the air like a pillow? One thing he did know, after tonight he'd be able to take any shortcut through town he wanted.

As unexplainable as all of that had been it paled in comparison to the encounter with that corpse-like man. Everything about him was unnatural, his greyish skin, his skull face, Sam could have sworn his eyes were yellow- and what made him freeze on the spot the way he had? Who was he, and what did he want with Sam? When he got back he'd find Miss Sarah and tell her everything, though he doubted she'd believe a word of it.

As he reached the city limits he could see smoke billowing over the treetops. The Foundry closed over an hour ago, so why were the smokestacks still going? Distant shouting could be heard along with what sounded like explosions coming from the other side of the hills. His worn shoes clapped the dirt road as he ran, the smoke growing darker than he'd seen the stacks push out on even the toughest days.

Moving the rest of the way at a full sprint, Sam reached the top and looked down at the city below. Though the sun had gone Farstone blazed with light, as fire tore through the ramshackle town. The streets were flooded with screaming townsfolk as houses collapsed in glowing orange heaps, flames pouring from blackened brick windows. Sam watched in horror as one of the Foundry's smokestacks toppled backward, the pillar of brick smashing through the roof the main warehouse.

Disbelief left him struck still until he heard a rustling in the brush beside him. He swept up a branch from the ground and held it over his shoulder like a club. As he did strange sensation washed over him, a warm prickling growing in the pit of his stomach that began to extend through his arms and legs. The feeling was unusual but welcome, he felt alert, sharp, like he could handle whatever waited in that brush without the slightest chance of failure.

He stood firm, stick raised to strike, when something crashed into him from behind. The stick flew from his hands as he was pinned beneath his assailant on the leaf strewn ground. He pushed a leathery mass off himself and fumbled for the stick when a voice spoke, hushed and irritated.

"What's the matter with you? Watch where you're going!"

Sam shook his head and looked up. A young woman was standing beside him, massaging her side with an irritated face. She couldn't have been more than a year or two older than him, her mass of red hair strewn with leaves and twigs from the ground. There was an intensity to her presence as she loomed over him, her eyes a bright, fierce green.

"Who are you? What are you doing out here?" She took a step back from him with her nose crumpled. "Why do you smell like an outhouse?"

She wore a form-fitting leather tunic held together with thick, uneven stitching and heavy brass buckles and rivets. Her trousers were similar, bound with a thick belt at her waist with a large ornate clasp. Heavy black boots were strapped to her feet, both splattered with grey mud. When he didn't respond she seized him by his collar and yanked him up with surprising strength.

"Well?"

His mouth went dry under her imposing glare. "S-Sam, my name's Sam."

"Were you captured too? Are there any of them out here?"

"Any of what out here? What are you talking about?"

"Joan!"

The voice made the two of them whirl around. The girl gave a delighted gasp as a young boy pushed his way through the brush, dressed in worn leather clothing like hers. His short crop of hair was the same burning red as the girl's, his eyes a light, watery hazel. His

37

freckled face was pale and fearful, clutching the older girl with dirty, quaking hands.

"Thomas!" She brushed his hair with her hand, examining his frightened face. "I was so worried- are you alright?

The boy nodded, quivering. He noticed Sam intruding on their reunion, giving him a look that was somewhere between scared and challenging. "Who's he? Where's Rand?"

"Rand can worry about himself. Come on, we need to get away before they find us."

Without a word to Sam the two of them ran off into the trees. Out of sheer impulse Sam chased after them, away from the burning city and into the surrounding hills.

"Wait! Where are you going?"

The two siblings moved fast, flipping over logs and boulders that blocked their path like a pair of acrobats. Sam struggled to follow, the smoke starting to spread through the trees. After a few minutes of chase the boy and girl came to a stop in a small clearing, the sister looking angered, the brother terrified.

"Get lost, kid! Can't you see we're trying to escape here?"

"Escape from what?" Sam asked, fighting to catch his breath. "What's going on here?"

"What's going on is that we're all in serious danger, and if you have any brains you'll clear out of here now. Let's go, Thomas."

The girl and her brother turned to leave when a howl shattered the night air like glass. Sam could see pearly shapes moving in the smoke between the trees, gleaming in the moonlight like pale specters. Six white wolves slid into the clearing, their breath steaming through their yellowed fangs. In a moment the beasts had them surrounded, black eyes fixed on their prey as they circled.

The three of them were back to back, turning slowly as the white demons closed in. The boy gave his sister a fearful look, who returned it with one of determination. "It's alright, it's just like we've practiced back home. You," she gave Sam a stiff elbow. "When I say duck, you'd better duck."

"Wha-"

"Duck!"

The first wolf lunged, fangs snapping like a steel press. Sam screamed and dropped to his knees, slipping under its bound by inches. Barely a second passed before another was on him, its foaming jaws trained on his back. The girl charged the wolf head-on, leaping and delivering a kick to the beast's midriff. Her thin leg should have buckled against the wall of fur and muscle, but the kick sent the wolf flying across the clearing into a thick evergreen.

Incredulous, Sam looked up to see her standing over him with her fists raised, hair falling over her face, her emerald eyes blazing. He tried to stand but she held him down, keeping her attention on the advancing wolves.

"Let us handle this."

A second wolf leapt in, rearing up on its hind legs with an awful snarl. Joan dropped low and swept its legs with almost blinding speed. Before it hit the ground she grabbed its tail and heaved the beast across the clearing into one of its fellows. Another closed in on the boy, who stood his ground, planting his feet in the dirt. When the wolf was close enough he thrust out a small hand, seizing its throat and jerking its head sideways. Its neck snapped with a crunch, the wolf slumping into the mud with its tongue lolling out.

Sam sat in amazement, his mouth gaping as he watched the siblings fight. The brother and sister ducked and dodged the savage attacks, moving almost too fast for Sam to see. Two of the wolves managed to box the girl against a tree, leaving her cornered. They howled and charged, but this time she made no move to defend herself. She closed her eyes and took a deep breath, standing still and calm in the face of certain death.

Fang and claw were nearly on her when she thrust out her arms, and Sam's jaw dropped as a plume of fire erupted from her palms. The wolves vanished into the flames, howling and whining for only a moment before dropping at her feet in two charred, smoking lumps. Sam rubbed his eyes as the girl swayed where she stood, looking suddenly uneasy on her feet.

Her brother shouted as another wolf lunged at her from behind. She turned as the beast tackled her to the ground, slashing her cheek with its heavy paw. The boy's arm shot out as he rushed in to help, but the other wolf dove at him and knocked him beside his sister. Sam sat helpless as the wolves closed in on them, covering his eyes to avoid witnessing the carnage.

The hairs on Sam's neck stood as snow fell, faster and more suddenly than he'd ever seen in his life. Wind buffeted him from all directions as powdery frost began swirling throughout the clearing. The two wolves reared back to strike and Sam covered his face, the beast's howls carrying through the blinding wind. As quickly as it started the miniature blizzard subsided and Sam looked between his fingers, coated from head to toe in white dust.

The wolves stood on their hind legs, both of them frozen in place. Frost in their fur gave it the true appearance of snow, their eyes like steamy black marbles. Beneath them were two snowy mounds where the brother and sister lay moments before. Sam slowly rose, brushing snow from his coat, and jumped when he heard another voice behind him.

"What would you do without me?"

Sam spun around to see a young man leaning against a tree, a scowl on his thin, pale face. His black hair was drawn back in a braided ponytail that hung over his shoulder, a few stray strands hanging down his forehead. He wore a white shirt and a light blue vest piped with silver thread, his dark pants tucked into tall cuffed boots. His clothing looked expensive, even regal, but was frayed and dirty from overuse. The young man approached the frozen wolves and ran a forefinger down a long, yellowed fang. Sam stared at the newcomer, unsure of what to make of him.

"W-who are you?"

The young man ignored him as he looked down at where Joan and Thomas lay buried, shaking his head and smirking. He reached into the snow and plucked them from it like carrots, dropping them once they were free.

"About time," Joan said, helping her brother up. When she straightened Sam noticed three deep gashes in her cheek where the wolf struck her, blood striping the side of her face. She didn't seem to notice, her attention on the older boy. "What kept you?"

"What kept me?" The young man gave her a contemptuous look. "You ran off the moment we escaped. You're lucky I found you when I did," His eyes lowered to her cheek. "I was about to move along without you." He rounded on Sam, his pale blue eyes piercing him. "And who is this?"

Another distant howl sounded in the dark. Joan's eyes raked the surrounding trees, her hands held in front of her. "We need to move, Rand."

"Agreed," the older boy said, and ran into the trees.

The brother and sister raced after him, Sam doing his best to keep up. He'd never gone this far from the city, following them through the woods for what had to be miles. Deep in the hills they came across a small cavern, and after a quick check for pawprints Rand ushered them inside. He held out his hands and ice began to form on the jagged stone until the entryway sealed, leaving a small airway at the top.

Joan took some dried brush from the cave floor and arranged it in a little pile. A thin stream of flame issued from her fingertips and the sticks ignited, the smoke trailing out of the vent in the ice. Her brother hung at her side, slight and silent in her shadow. Sam looked at the three of them, more confused than ever.

"Who are you guys?"

"You're the stranger here," Rand said. "Who are you, exactly?"

41

"We ran into him right after we broke away," Joan answered. "Pretty sure he's a local from the mortal city."

"Is this true?" Rand asked.

Sam didn't understand. 'Mortal city?' "I'm from here, if that's what you mean," He pointed his thumb over his shoulder at the cave's mouth. "I live at the Orphanage in Farstone."

Rand looked solemn. "Fortunate for you that you weren't there when it happened. Had you been, you'd be dead... or worse."

"When what happened?" Sam asked.

"When the army attacked," Rand said in a dark voice.

"What army?"

"The army of undead."

Sam was silent for a moment, then snickered to himself. Rand looked grave as he watched Sam break into laughter. "Is something amusing here?"

"Alright, alright, I know what's going on now. Boy, Len must have really clocked me good." He closed his eyes and shook his head, expecting to wake up on his back between Stone & Stone and Martin's any moment. "Fighting wolves, shooting fire, the snowstorm- Let me guess, you guys must be the Strong, right?"

Sam stopped laughing when he noticed the others weren't smiling in the slightest. The three of them were now looking at him like he was one of the pearly white wolves. Joan stepped right through the fire and seized him by the coat, lifting him off his feet.

"What are you doing?" Sam stammered. "Let me go!"

"He's a spy! He'll lead him right to us!"

"What are you talking about? Put me down!"

Rand stood beside Joan, glaring at him with blackness. "Explain, then, how a scrawny boy from a mortal city knows anything about the ancient bloodline of the Strong?"

"This!"

Sam fumbled in his coat, still dangling from Joan's fist, and held up the book. Rand swiped it from him and began thumbing through the pages. Joan still held him tight, her eyes dark with menace.

"Remarkable," Rand said, his blue eyes wide as he flipped through the pages. "This must be hundreds of years old, it could even predate the Schism..." He looked at Sam in wonder. "Where on earth did you get this?"

"It's from my parents! Let me go!"

"Your parents?" Rand looked astounded.

"What is it?" Joan asked.

"Drop him," Rand commanded. Joan scowled but released her grip, dropping Sam onto the hard floor. The older boy looked intently at Sam. "You're an orphan, you say? An orphan from this Farstone place?"

"Yes," Sam replied, his backside sore from the landing.

"And this, this was left to you by your parents?" Rand held up the book, soot from the cover blackening his fingers.

Sam nodded. Joan looked from Sam to Rand in aggravated confusion. "What is it already?"

Rand lowered the book and leaned toward Sam, extending a hand to help him. Sam took it and got to his feet, uncertain of what was going to happen next. Rand looked at the two others, their unsure faces shadowed in firelight. He smoothed back his long hair and took a deep breath, then spoke to Sam in a commanding but measured tone.

"I am Rand of the Northern Kingdom. Joan and Thomas here are from the mountain realm of Everhearth in the west. Our homelands were attacked and destroyed by an army of undead warriors, and I'm afraid they've just done the same to yours."

Sam couldn't believe what he was hearing. "Undead?"

"Yes," Rand said. "They are the creations of a vile creature, a reaper of souls, a tyrant of the grave, the most evil of our kind to ever walk this world- a necromancer. In short, these evil Strong use their dark power to-"

43

"Raise the dead," Sam finished. "There's a story about them in my book. I thought they were wiped out?"

Rand looked uncomfortable with the amount of knowledge Sam had about the Strong, but kept his commanding composure. "Their sect was destroyed long ago, yes, but some remnant of their black magic remained hidden. After centuries this evil has been uncovered, and a new Dark One has risen. He is eradicating the Strong and transforming them into legions of his horrors. He will not rest until he has taken every last one of us, down to the last child."

Sam remembered the man from the alley. "I saw him! Just now back in the alley, he wanted me to follow him but I ran for it. That's when I bumped into them," He pointed at the brother and sister.

"You didn't see the Dark One," Joan said. "If you did you wouldn't be alive to talk about it."

"Well, he sure looked undead," Sam recalled the chill he'd felt in the man's presence. "He told me his name was Bones."

"Yes, one of his lieutenants, the leader of one of his armies," Rand looked at Joan and Thomas. "We've been his prisoners for nearly two months. Before his forces attacked your city he set out to case the area and we were able to escape. That vile half-demon is almost as evil and cruel as his master."

"So... it's true?"

He looked around at his three new companions, his mouth dry, his whole body shaking. "The stories, the powers, the Strong... it's all real?"

"Well, yes," Rand answered. "Did you not hear a thing I just said?"

"So..." Sam spoke slowly, "If that book was left with me by my family... then does that mean..."

"Let me ask you this," Rand said. "Have there any signs of power that set you apart, some extraordinary physical talent or skill for instance?"

"Not by the looks of it," Joan said.

Sam scowled. "So I'm not the biggest or toughest kid around, being smart counts more than any of that."

"I'd believe you were tough before I believed you were smart," she remarked.

Sam was about to give her a suggestion of where to go when he noticed the cuts on her cheek, which were already beginning to close. He didn't know why it hadn't come to him sooner.

"My whole life, whenever I've gotten beat up I heal in a few hours, no matter how bad it was. Black eyes, bruises, even a broken nose once, I'll go to sleep and wake up good as new. The nurses from the Orphanage could never explain it."

"A discerning trait in Strong," Rand said, nodding. "Our bodies are far less susceptible to physical damage than mortal flesh."

"And tonight," Sam said, the evening's events replaying in his head. "These kids attacked me, and something happened... I was really fast, and strong... I beat them up like it was nothing, three kids twice my size. Well, two were twice my size..."

Rand nodded once more. "Our power can awaken in times of intense stress or conflict."

Sam could still see the book in the flaming barrel. "So it's... it's awakened in me, or whatever? I'm really a Strong?"

"Hold on a minute," Joan said, looking at Rand. "Are you trying to tell me this little weasel is actually one of us?"

"It is faint, but I can feel the power in him," Rand said. "And *I* am certainly not one of *you.*"

Sam wasn't listening to them. He was staring at his own hands, his whole body shaking. "This is incredible!"

He snatched up a rock from the cave floor and squeezed, trying to crush it in his grip. When it didn't break he tried two hands, pushing with all his might, but the rock remained hard and unyielding as the cave walls around him.

"What's wrong?" Sam let the rock clatter to the floor. "Why can't I break it?"

"You have no control over your power," Rand said. "You experienced a fleeting burst when you needed to save yourself-"

"Show me, then!" Sam couldn't contain his excitement. "I want to learn everything-"

"You don't get it, do you?" Joan's voice echoed in the small cavern. "The Dark One is hunting Strong, which puts you in the same danger it puts us. He and his monsters will kill you the first chance they get!"

"Isn't there anything we can do to stop him?" Sam asked.

Rand chuckled. "Impossible. He has hordes of undead that grow each day, and power greater than any Strong alive. We could never hope to stop him."

"What about the other Strong? There are still other king-doms, aren't there?"

"Even if there are, it makes no difference to us. The Strong kingdoms have been lost to one another for centuries. We could never hope to find one."

"What if we had maps?"

Sam took the book and flipped to the back section where the maps of the different kingdoms were drawn. Rand's jaw dropped, snatching it back again and gaping at the page.

"This is astounding," His finger ran back and forth across the maps. "My own kingdom is noted here!"

"Let me see that," Joan stretched out to grab the book. "If ours is in there I'm torching it."

"Go ahead and try," Sam took the book back from Rand and held it up to the three of them. "Think about it, we can use this to find the other kingdoms, and warn the Strong so they can be prepared to fight. Who knows, maybe we can get them to join forces? We may be able to stop this necromancer!"

"Forget it," Joan said. "I'm not risking us getting captured again to save some sorry other Strong we don't owe a thing."

"It would be exceedingly dangerous," Rand said, though his eyes remained locked on the pages.

Joan looked at Sam and shrugged. "Sorry, kid, but the adventure ends here. Come daybreak Thomas and I are out of here."

"Where are you going to go?" Sam asked. "What if they find you?"

"Don't you worry about us, we'll make our own way. Have fun with your little plan if you want, but we're not interested in being part of some suicide mission."

"Come on, we could do this," Sam persisted. "If someone had warned your kingdom you might still be there, wouldn't you?"

This time Joan had no remark. Silence filled the cavern, except for the crackling of the fire. They all looked away from each other, Rand at the book, Joan the fire, Thomas the floor, and Sam the ice door.

"I'll do it."

Three heads turned to Rand. He had a purposeful, knowing expression on his face, his eyes moving from face to face. "We cannot sit by and allow the world to fall to this evil. If we are the only ones who can help then it is our duty to do so."

"You've got to be joking," Joan said. "You're actually buying this?"

"The boy has a point," Rand said. "There is nowhere for you to go, they will never stop hunting you. You will never find safety for you and your brother while these creatures roam the world."

"We'll take our chances," Joan said.

"Don't you care that this he's going to do the same thing to the rest of the Strong he did to you?" Sam said, his words close to pleading.

"Like I said, not interested."

"Let them run," Rand gave her a lofty look. "I knew you Westerners weren't known to be the brightest or most civilized, but I never took you for cowards."

Smoke issued from Joan's palms as she seethed at Rand, who didn't falter for a moment. "You're free to go your own way, but I am not afraid. I will go on this quest alone if I have to."

"Hey, it was my idea," Sam interjected. "And in case you forgot, it's my book."

Rand gave him an appraising look. "You think you're ready for this?"

"Are you kidding? I know this thing like the back of my hand. You're going to need me on this one for sure!"

"I would hardly say 'need'," The older boy sounded smug. "But I suppose being the book's owner earns you the right."

Sam was brimming with excitement. "I can't believe this, my own Strong adventure!"

"Give me a break," Joan sneered. "You nearly wet yourself at a few wolves. You think you're ready to fight these monsters?"

"Every hand helps," Rand noted, eyes lingering on Sam's book. "Not everyone's strengths are physical, after all."

"They're right, Joan," Thomas suddenly looked up at his sister, his voice small but steady. "I think we should do this. It's what Father would want."

The boy had been so quiet the entire time that Sam almost forgot he was sitting there. Joan stared at her brother for a minute, her green eyes searching his freckled face. Defeated, she threw her hands in the air. "I can't believe I'm doing this."

"It's settled then," Sam said, holding out a fist shaking with excitement. "Let's make an oath right now: we'll stop at nothing to defeat the necromancer, or Dark One, or whoever he is. We won't stop until we've saved the Strong!"

"I admire your enthusiasm," Rand extended his knuckles to Sam's with a derisive look. "If nothing else."

The two of them turned to the siblings, the boy's small fist joining theirs immediately. The sister hesitated, then after a pointed face from her brother she too put her hand in. "I hope you're happy," she said to him.

"That will do for now," Rand said. "Let's try and get some rest."

He turned his hand toward the fire and extinguished it with a quick blast of snow. Sam settled on the least lumpy section of the cave floor he could find, balling his coat into a pillow. He didn't know how he was expected to sleep after everything that had happened, and the thought of what was about to come. From the moment he'd heard the Foundry cancelled shifts he should've known this was going to be no ordinary day.

# V

"Wake up," A rough hand jostled Sam awake. He recoiled, expecting Agatha cocking back the switch, but instead of the old woman he saw a blur of red. It was then realized that he wasn't lying in his cot but on a hard cave floor. There were no other cots beside him, no barred windows above his head, only cold rock walls and a charred pile of ash.

He sat up, his shoulder aching where Joan had shaken him. There were streaks of dried blood on the girl's cheek but the scratches the wolf left had healed completely. The sheet of ice was gone, replaced by a muddy puddle at the cave's mouth. Rand and Thomas waited at the entrance, the older boy standing with impatience while the other looked away, hunched and quiet.

"Let's get moving," Rand said. "We've no time to waste."

Sam picked up the book and followed the others away from the cave. He took one last look in the direction of Farstone, a grey plume still rising over the hills. He had no love lost for his life in the miserable city, but the townspeople didn't deserve such a horrible fate. He thought of Miss Sarah, the other kids from the Orphanage, even Agatha... he didn't want to bring himself to think what might have become of them.

"Bones has to have noticed we're gone by now," Rand said as morning grew around them. "He'll make finding us as much a priority as hunting the other Strong. If his master finds out he let us escape, Bones will find himself among the ranks of the army instead of leading it."

"Do you think he'll find us?" Sam asked.

"Probably, if we keep moving so slow," Joan glared at him at the back of the group.

"He is leading his forces east," Rand continued, "Before the attack I overheard him telling one of his underlings that they were headed towards water."

"So shouldn't we be heading in the exact opposite direction?" Joan said.

"If he's heading that way, it means there is another kingdom that way," Rand's tone suggested annoyance at her inability to piece together the obvious. "I'll have a look around and see what I can find."

He leapt up twice his height and grabbed a thick branch, scaling the rest of the nearly fifty foot tree in moments. Joan followed up the tree beside it, leaving Sam and Thomas to wait at their roots. The younger boy hadn't said a word since their pact in the cave the night before. He stood small and timid against the tree, like a fawn separated from its mother.

"That was really something, you and your sister with those wolves last night," Sam tried to fill the silence with small talk. "I've never seen anyone fight like that. How old are you?"

"Eleven," Thomas answered in a quiet voice, eyes down.

"I'm not sure how old I am exactly," Sam said. "I think I'm thirteen, but I might be fourteen by now, who knows? You don't know your birthday when you're left at an orphanage, do you?"

He gave a nervous laugh. Thomas didn't respond, eyes still fixed on the dirt. Sam whistled, rocking on his heels, then tried taking the conversation in another direction. "So, you and your sister are from Everhearth, huh?"

No answer. Sam tried continuing. "There's a story about it in my book, I've read all about it. It's a city built into a volcano, right? That sounds pretty-"

"Is he bothering you, Thomas?"

Joan landed with a thud behind Sam, leaving a shallow crater in the ground. The boy looked up at his sister and shook his head. Joan gave Sam a hard look. "Leave him alone, alright? He's been through enough, he doesn't need some numbskull like you badgering him with stupid questions."

Rand landed beside Sam, lighter but with enough force to indent the dirt at his feet. "Well, no sign of Bones, thankfully. I could make out a sea to the east as well, thirty miles from here give or take."

"Hey, I'm the one who spotted it," Joan said.

Rand ignored her. "Bones will be forced to lead his army around, which will take at least a week. If we cross the sea by boat it would put us days ahead of him."

Sam looked excited. "We're getting on a ship?"

"It's our best option," Rand said. "From there we'll try to use that book of yours to find the next kingdom before Bones does."

"Let's hope you're right," Joan said with a shake of her head. "I'm saying it now, this is a bad idea."

The four young Strong moved quick across the hilly terrain, covering the thirty miles in only a few hours' time. Sam lagged behind the others but noticed a spring in his step that had never been there before. He'd been running all morning and still felt refreshed and alert, his breath still steady in his lungs. His aches and pains from the Foundry were replaced with an invigorating warmth that seemed to radiate from the others, pulling him along with them like a leaf in the wind's hold.

Shortly after midday the scent of salt reached Sam's nose, the rhythmic thrum of water on rocks growing in the distance. They passed the last few trees and came to a bare cliffside overlooking a vast green sea. A sign hung from a dead tree poking from the cliff's edge, swaying in the salty breeze. Sam inspected the weather-beaten lettering, brushing away the caked sand covering it.

It pointed to a path leading to the cliff's base, where dozens of drab buildings were arranged by a large array of boat docks. Ships of varying sizes and styles were docked there, looking like toys from their height.

"I've heard of this place," Sam said, pointing at the sign. "It's supposed to be one the biggest merchant ports on the coast. The Foundry sends goods there to ship to overseas buyers. Sounds like exactly what we need!"

They made their way down the steep, rocky path until they reached the outskirts of Bale's Cove. After passing a few seaside cottages the buildings quickly condensed into a dingy port town mobbed with people, all of them either buying or selling. Everywhere merchants were haggling at their stands, peddling everything from fine fragrances to fish heads. Dozens of boats rocked in the foaming water beside a dock that seemed to stretch right to the horizon.

"What a dump," Joan remarked, looking around at the sandy streets and wind-beaten buildings. "This place looked a lot better from up there."

"It's a step up from Knot Street, that's for sure," Sam watched two rats squabble over a hunk of moldy bread beneath a wooden cart. "I just hope we don't run into any of Bones'-"

Before he finished Joan slugged him in the shoulder with the force of a grown man. He grunted and whirled toward her, rubbing his arm. "What was that for?"

"Are you trying to get us caught?" Joan whispered. "The Dark One's supposed to have spies all over, you never know who might be listening to us, even here. Don't mention Bones, necromancers or anything to do with any of it, got it?"

Rand was looking towards the docks, standing on his toes to see over the crowd. "We're going to have to get on one of these."

"How do you plan on doing that?" Joan asked. "They're not going to ferry us across out of the goodness of their hearts. Where are we going to get money?"

"I know a few ways of getting some quick loot," Sam said, eyeing a passerby's coin satchel dangling from her waist.

"We won't stoop to petty theft," Rand said. "Besides, the last thing we need is to draw attention to ourselves."

"I think it's a little late for that," Joan said with a pointed nod. Some of the port's inhabitants were taking notice of their unusual dress, some looking politely curious or amused, others wary, scrutinizing. A group of joking kids came through the crowd and giggled when they noticed the four of them, nudging each other and pointing.

"Get a load of these guys," One of them laughed, pointing at Rand as they passed. "Nice vest, pal!"

"We're sticking out like burnt thumbs," Joan said as an old woman watched her with nosy interest. "I knew this was a bad idea."

"Let's just find a ship heading east," Rand said. "It won't matter once we're aboard."

They made their way toward the docks, the salty air mingling with the pungent stench of sweat. The area was filled with the shouts and grunts as dozens of dockhands toiled around them. Everywhere sails were being pulled in or cast out, men shimmied up and down ropes nimbly as spiders. Most of the ships had gangplanks leading down to the dock, each manned by someone exchanging money for tickets.

Sam was trying to see over the crowd when he noticed a shabby-looking tramp by a merchant cart watching him with wide, wild eyes. He might have been close to thirty, but his thick beard gave him the appearance of a man years older. His black hair was long and unkempt, falling to the shoulders of his long, worn over-coat. He and Sam locked eyes, and Sam saw the pair looking back was a piercing, unnatural grey.

He turned away and hurried behind the others, feeling a sense of unease. Joan watched a man pass a handful of coins to one of the ticket collectors, who examined them under his wide brimmed hat. Once he was satisfied he pocketed the silver and handed the man a crisp yellow ticket. As the man boarded another stepped forward, only to be turned away when the ticket collector counted his money.

Joan turned to Rand. "Now what?"

"There's more than one way to get aboard," Rand said with a note of impatience. "Ships are always taking on cabin hands. I'll bet if we talk with one of the shipmates we can work off our passage on the way."

"There's no way I'm peeling potatoes and cleaning out bed-pans," Joan stated, and Thomas gave a small nod of agreement. "There's got to be another way. Any ideas, Smelly?"

She turned to Sam expecting a retort, but he wasn't standing behind her anymore. He was weaving his way through the crowd to get a better view of the ships. He marveled at the magnificent ves-sels, taking in the cloudlike sails and fine woodworking. One in par-ticular caught his eye, a fine three-masted ship with a beautiful fig-urehead at its bow. Her hair was carved in golden curls around her face, hands clutched against her chest, her painted eyes staring mournfully into his.

He was so engrossed in the ship he didn't notice where he was walking, and bumped into a burly dockhand carrying a length of thick rope. "Watch where you're going, you stinkin' bilge rat! Can't you see we're working here?"

"Sorry," Sam stammered, looking up into the man's agitated face.

"This is no place for kids, now go on, scat!"

Sam started walking off when he noticed two men rolling barrels down another narrow gangplank leading into the ship's cargo hold. A third man was standing by a stack of barrels, chatting with a woman in a green hoop skirt, a matching parasol blooming on her shoulder. He leaned on an empty barrel, sitting beside a cart of lumpy red potatoes.

"No, no, this isn't my *real* job," the man twirled his long mustache with a grin. "I'm just doing a favor for a friend, poor man's sick as a dog. I'm a helmsman by trade, one of the best there is!"

The woman batted her lashes. "How impressive!"

"That's right, I've sailed every corner of this sea, fought countless storms, there's none better on these docks than me, my dear!"

"There you are," An agitated voice spoke behind Sam. He turned and saw Joan and the others. "What are you doing over here?"

"I think I have an idea," he said, his eyes on the empty barrel. "Follow me."

They crept around the side of the cart, careful not to draw the attention of the other workers. The man stood with his back to them, oblivious to anything but the pretty eyes in front of him. Sam motioned to the others towards a row of empty barrels waiting to be filled by the oblivious dockhand.

"Are you crazy?" Joan whispered. "That'll never-"

"Oi, Simon!" One of the men loading the barrels shouted at the fawning man. "If you want to get paid for the day you'll keep those barrels coming!"

"Alright, alright!" The man called back, then whirled back to the woman. "Sorry, if you could just give me a moment."

"Of course," The parasol twirled on her shoulder. "I'd love to hear some of your sea tales."

Sam looked around the cart and saw the man hastily filling barrels with potatoes. The woman still had his complete attention, and he dropped a heap of spuds onto the ground. He grumbled as he stooped to pick them up, and Sam dashed forward and hopped into an empty barrel. There was a shuffling sound, and then he felt the barrels on either side of his wobble just as the man stepped beside them.

"That's right, that wave must've been a hundred, no, two hundred feet tall! Guided my ship right up it and down the back just before it swallowed us up. Yep, saved a lot of lives that day, I did!"

Sam curled into a ball and closed his eyes, hoping to the heavens this would work. He could hear the man right outside the barrel, still braying to the woman, as a pile of potatoes rained down over his head. The barrel went dark as the man sealed the lid, then he lurched forward as the barrel was turned on its side and began rolling. He came to a stop and was stood back up, and Sam could hear different voices outside.

"Simon's at it again, the bloody fool."

"What's it this time? The hundred foot wave again?"

"Two hundred this time. Hell of an imagination he's got, don't he?"

"He'll sure have plenty of time to make more of that stuff up while he's peeling these below deck the whole trip."

Both laughed and Sam was rolling again. The barrel moved several more feet and was turned back on its end, only now Sam's head was on the bottom. He could hear and feel other barrels being loaded as a cramp started developing in his neck. There was a loud scrape of the gangplank being pulled away, followed by the boom of the cargo door sealing.

He waited a few more minutes before he shifted his weight and tipped himself over. The lid popped free he crawled out, cracking and craning his neck. He looked around the dark, wide room, light peeking in from portholes near the cargo door. The room was packed with large wooden crates with their contents marked in stenciled lettering, spare sections of sail and rope, and dozens of identical barrels neatly stacked in rows of three.

A whistle screeched in the distance and the ship lurched, and Sam could hear men shouting above as they disembarked. The floor rocked beneath his feet, the barrels and crates creaking and swaying. A few rows down from him a barrel was wiggling at the bottom of its stack. He struggled to get the two barrels off the first, which tipped once it was free. Boots kicked out the bottom and Joan came squirming out, curls of potato caught on the rivets of her tunic.

Rand popped out of a top barrel a few rows down and leapt to the floor. With one hand Joan lifted two barrels and pried open the bottom one with the other. She reached in and helped her brother out, who looked up at her with his eyes crossed, looking dazed.

"I can't believe that worked," Rand said. "That was quick thinking, Sam."

"Pure luck," Joan said. "Let's clean this up and get out of here before we get caught."

They collected the strewn potatoes and resealed their barrels, stacking them back in their places. Outside the storage room a salty breeze and the call of gulls drew them to a staircase leading to the deck. Shipmates dragged ropes and hoisting sails as they guided the ship from the port. Passengers were hanging over the railings as the ship cast off, some waving to friends and family on the pier, others looking over the starboard side at the horizon.

Rand looked up and down the ship, his blue eyes scanning the deck. "It shouldn't take us more than a day or two to reach the east coast. If our luck holds we'll pass unnoticed."

"That's going to be tough looking like we do," Joan said. "We should've found some different clothes while we were in town."

"I don't think it will be that big of a problem. Ports see all sorts of foreigners and travelers."

"Yeah, but most travelers aren't trying to hide from..." There was no need for her to finish. "We should've just stayed in those barrels until we reached the port."

"And what if someone opened them while we were inside? We'd be arrested as stowaways!"

"At least we'd be safe from *them* finding us. I'd take a few days in the brig over that."

Sam swayed where he stood, grabbing Joan's shoulder for balance. She pushed him off and he stumbled, his face pale, slacken. Rand reached out a hand and shook him by the shoulder. "Are you alright?"

Sam didn't answer, his eyes closed, lips quivering. Joan glanced nervously around the deck. "You don't think-"

She seized him by the front of his coat, her green eyes wide. "Kid, are you still there? Is he in your head?" She gave him a hard shake. "Answer me!"

Sam pushed her aside and staggered over to the ship's edge. He clutched the railing with both hands, then leaned over the side and hurled.

"That's him alright," Joan turned away as Sam hung over the ship's edge, his legs kicking as he retched. "We're doomed."

# VI

Taking to the seas seemed exciting when they first arrived at Bale's Cove, but now Sam couldn't wait to return to shore. He'd spent the better part of the morning leaning over the starboard side, as well as most of the night before. His face was green as he clutched the railing, trying to keep himself still against the ship's constant swaying. Wiping his mouth on his sleeve, he looked up when he heard two sets of footsteps approaching from behind.

"Thinking of jumping?"

It was Joan and Thomas, the girl actually looking amused for once. "It looks like you're enjoying your trip so far."

"How much longer is this going to take?" Sam asked, covering his mouth as he fought to keep his stomach at bay.

"I heard a couple of deckhands talking," Joan said. "If the weather holds we should reach the eastern port by sundown."

Sam groaned, looking back over the railing with a grimace. "I don't know how much more of this I can take."

The girl smirked. "You couldn't wait to get on a ship, remember? Come on, let's hit the galley, some food might settle your stomach."

As they made their way across the deck Sam saw the bearded tramp from the docks, watching them as he leaned against the ship's railing. Sam held his grey gaze for a moment before turning away, then gave Joan a furtive nudge.

"That's the guy I was telling you about, the one I saw back on the docks."

Joan didn't look but gave a slight nod. "I've noticed him, too. He was skulking around while Thomas and I watched the sunset last night."

"You don't think he's-?"

"Whoever he is, he'd better mind his own business if he knows what's good for him."

The bravado was obvious in her voice. Sam could tell she felt just as uneasy about their mysterious tail as he did. He glanced back and felt a small relief when he saw the stranger had turned away, now looking at the horizon with the same wildness in his eyes.

They descended the stairs to the ship's lower level, an open room filled with laughing and drinking passengers. A queue had formed along one wall where a toothless cook ladled a foul smelling stew out to anyone brave enough to try it. They each took a bowl and noticed Rand sitting alone at a nearby table, reading the book. A group of boisterous men played cards at the table beside him, squabbling over the outcome of each hand in a flurry of slurred cursing.

"Something smells like vomit," Rand said as they joined him, not taking his eyes off the book. Sam took a sudden interest in a knothole on the table as Joan smirked in his direction. He spoke before she had the chance to. "There's some great stuff in there, huh? Did you get to the part with the emerald chest yet?"

"He hasn't put it down since you gave it to him," Joan said. "How about we forget storytime for a minute and figure out our next move?"

"There's an incredible amount of history in this book. If we stand any chance at finding the other kingdoms we'll need to learn everything we can about them. Of course, I shouldn't expect a cave-dwelling savage to show any interest in the academic."

Joan's spoon creaked as she jabbed at her lumpy stew. Sam pushed his own bowl aside, convinced there was something swimming in it. Rand was flipping back and referencing one of the first few pages, looking confused.

"Looking for something?" Sam asked. "I know every story by heart."

"I'm trying to figure out where we'll find the nearest kingdom. Early in the book there's a tale about a dangerous wood called-"

"The Sharpwood Forest," Sam supplied. "A place so dangerous even the trees attacked you."

"Indeed," Rand continued. "The story tells of an adventurer who stumbled upon a tribe of Strong living deep in this forest, in a lost village carved into the trees. They were master archers and swordsmen, and experts of stealth and ambushes. It says that a Sharpwood warrior can be all but invisible if given just the smallest branch to hide behind."

"Sounds like the kind of guys we're looking for," Joan said, grabbing the book from him and flipping through it. "Now let's see the map and plan our route."

Sam put his hand over the book to stop Joan ravaging its pages. "The Sharpwood warriors were the most isolated Strong of all. They didn't want any more outsiders finding their secret kingdom, so when the adventurer left he swore to never reveal their location to anyone."

"So there's no map?"

"Well, no, he-"

Joan let the book drop onto the table. "Then why mention it at all?"

"It's a great story," Sam said, picking the book up and brushing it off. "Epic battles, strange plants and creatures, at the end there's this gigantic-"

"It mentions something called the 'Red Ridge'," Rand cut through, tapping his finger on the page. "I saw the same name marked on the map Bones was following. If we head southeast from the next port, we should-"

Thomas looked alarmed, tugging at his sister's arm and nodding towards the wall. On the opposite side of the galley the wild-looking man was watching them from behind a pewter flagon. He set his drink down slow, grey eyes wide as he dabbed his lip on his frayed sleeve.

"What is it?" Rand asked.

"That guy over there's been eyeballing us since the docks," Joan said. "I don't like the look of him one bit."

"Hmm," Rand picked up Sam's spoon and wiped it with his thumb, taking a look behind him in its reflection. "Looks like your common drunken drifter to me."

"He could be a spy," Joan whispered.

"Let's not become paranoid," Rand said. "Even if he is, there's not much we can do until we reach the port. Besides, he's only a mortal. If it did come to it, I think we'd be more than capable of defending ourselves."

They turned their attention back to the book, combing it for more clues that might lead them to the Sharpwood Forest. Sam's unease soon changed to eagerness as they discussed their adventure, trying to keep their voices hushed. Passengers came and went, swaying either from the rocking of the ship or the ale in their hands. Sam felt better when he glanced back and saw that the man had disappeared, the flagon abandoned on the empty table.

The ship lurched and Sam's stool slid backwards into a passenger sitting behind him. The man grumbled and turned, his heavy red mustache drawn in a scowl. "Watch it!"

"Sorry," Sam said, sliding back to the table. The man grabbed his shoulder and stood up, looking down at him and the others.

"You'll be sorry if you don't watch yourself," The man's breath was ripe with rum. "You could've cost me the hand!"

"Hold on a minute," Another man at the table rose to his feet, eyes narrowed under the brim of his hat. "I don't remember taking tickets from any kids."

"We were some of the first aboard, sir," Rand answered in a calm voice. "We gave our tickets to another man."

"Let's see your ticket stubs, then," the man clutching Sam's shoulder said.

"Uh," Sam started to stammer, "I-I have it here somewhere, I think-"

"Don't lie!" Several passengers turned to look as the man in the hat pointed at the four of them. "I was the only one collecting tickets, I think I'd remember four kids gussied up in bloody strange clothes like that!"

The man with the mustache turned to his fellows as the rest of them rose to their feet. "Looks like we've got ourselves some stowaways, boys!"

"Lock 'em in the brig!" One of the others snarled.

The ship lurched again, hard this time, sending cards and mugs clattering to the floor. It rocked the other way, bowls and mugs breaking all across the galley. Sailors were cursing in annoyance while passengers looked nervously at the ceiling and one another. A thunderclap like a cannon blast boomed overhead and the ship bucked again, this time hard enough to knock several people to the floor. A deckhand came clamoring down the staircase, windswept and drenched from head to foot.

"The sky's opened up out here! We need all hands, let's go!"

The man released Sam as he and the others clamored after the deckhand. Everyone else followed suit, bowling over one another as they tried to make for the stairs. Sam turned back to the others when a passenger brushed passed him and knocked him to the floor. When he managed to get back up there was no sign of Rand, Joan, or Thomas. The pewter mug still rested on the table right where the grey-eyed man had left it.

He dashed up the stairs and onto the deck, already slick with driving rain. His eyes raked the swaying ship for the others as men seized ropes and pulleys to maneuver the whipping sails. He thought he saw the blue of Rand's vest when someone yanked him by the wrist. A deckhand brandished a thick rope at him, shouting at him over the storm. Sam recognized him as Simon, the boasting, mustached man from the docks.

"Hold this tight, boy! We're liable to tip any minute!"

"I-"

The man thrust the rope into Sam's hands and began operating a heavy crank on the mast, giving him no choice but to pull on the rapidly tightening rope. He held on as wind and rain whipped him from every angle, the rope's coarse fibers scratching his palms as he began to slide on the wet floor. Simon cranked the winch as hard as he could, shouting to Sam over the storm.

"Keep it tight, now!" The sailor's mustache was plastered to his face from the rain as he fought with the crank, yards of coiled rope at his feet. "Don't worry, I know what I'm doing, I've done this a hundred-"

The handle broke off in the man's hands and Sam fell back as the tension released. A loop of rope tightened around Simon's ankle and hoisted him to the top of the mast. His screams were swallowed by the storm as the ship rocked again, the rope snapping and launching him into the thrashing sea.

Sam scrambled away as the ship continued to buck, the deck boards starting to twist at his feet. A man came sprinting up the staircase from the lower level, shouting at the helmsman. "We're taking on water!"

"Get the lifeboats ready!" The helmsman gritted his teeth as he struggled to steady the wheel. Many passengers were already way ahead of him, battling one another for a spot in one of the tiny rafts. A blur of red caught Sam's eye as a bolt of lightning lit the darkness. At the opposite end of the ship were Rand, Joan and Thomas, the three working fast to free one of the lifeboats.

Lighting flashed again and he saw a figure approaching him, moving calmly despite the calamity of the situation. It was the bearded stranger, striding toward him with grimness in his grey eyes. Sam sprinted towards Joan and the others, who looked to be having difficulty freeing their boat. He'd nearly reached them when the ship bucked hard and knocked him back to the deck, and sent a few unlucky souls tumbling over the edge.

Sam clung to the railing, struggling to his feet as the deck grew steeper and steeper. The shadow of a massive wave loomed above them like a mountain, drawing the helpless ship up its sloping face. Sailors and passengers screamed in terror, fighting one another for a seat in one of the lifeboats, but they were useless. Sam's shoes left the floor as the ship went vertical, and with a roar of ocean and thunder the wave crested.

The water felt like brick as Sam was flung into the churning sea. He tumbled like a ragdoll, colliding with debris from the pulverized ship. Salt stung his eyes as he spun through the dark, unsure which way was up, then another bright flash showed him the surface. He kicked for the light when he felt a pull on his ankle like a hangman's noose. Through the brine he could see a length of chain had caught his leg, along with a healthy section of the ship's mast.

Sam kicked and pulled but he couldn't free himself, sinking deeper and deeper by the second. He had no idea how long he'd been holding his breath, his chest felt like it was going to explode...

The lightning above was growing dimmer and dimmer... Why, why did it have to end like this...

There was a jerk on the chain, and now he felt it pulling him fast to the surface. Sam gasped as he his face hit air and was heaved out of the water onto a hard, bobbing object. He sat up, choking and sputtering, and realized he was sitting in one of the lifeboats. A piece of chain was still around his ankle, and he saw the links at the end had been squished together like clay.

The tiny boat rocked and bucked against the angry waters, and Sam noticed with a jolt the other passengers. Joan and Thomas sat huddled together across from him, drenched and ghostly pale in the lightning. Rand gripped the opposite side of the boat, his eyes locked on the boat's fourth passenger. It was their mysterious bearded pursuer, guiding the tiny boat through the chaos.

"Hang on tight!"

His hand was wrapped around a rope tied to a makeshift sail, his grey eyes alight with wild pleasure as he fought the storm with unnatural ease. The others looked terrified as the boat started to climb another huge swell, but the man grinned and yanked hard on the rope. Sam squinted against another crash of lightning, his ears filled with screaming. Once he could see he too started screaming, as the boat careened headlong into the shore.

# VII

The rain pounding his head told Sam that he must still be alive, and the groans he heard meant the others probably made it, too. Their boat was wedged in a pit of sandy mud between two sharp boulders. One by one each of them leapt out of the splintered boat, Sam's right foot squashing in the mud. He must have lost his shoe in the commotion and not even noticed. He clutched at the front of his jacket and felt a rush of relief at the familiar rectangular outline still beneath it.

The stranger climbed from the boat onto one of the boulders. Rain dripped from his beard as he looked up and down the dark coastline. "Only missed the port by a mile or two," He spoke more to himself than any of them. "Not too shabby."

"Who are you?" Rand questioned him with demanding authority.

"Name's Jack," The stranger replied, his gaze still on the coast. Rand gave him a cold look and turned to the others, talking over the whipping wind. "We need to find shelter. These woods look thick enough to-"

The man turned and set off down the beach, holding his coat closed against the wind. The four of them watched him depart with confused, curious looks.

"Where are you going?" Sam called.

"To find an inn, and with any luck some good brandy. You're welcome to join me, unless you'd prefer a night under the stars."

He continued at a brisk pace, his figure diminishing in the driving rain. Sam turned to the others, each of them eyeing the man's retreating back. "Well?"

Joan raised an eyebrow. "Well what?"

"Should we go?"

"Go where?"

"He said he's going to an inn-"

Joan laughed. "You're not seriously thinking of following that guy, are you?"

"He just saved our lives-"

"You really are as dumb as you look. We can't just trust anyone we run into!"

"You trusted me," Sam muttered.

"Because you were so hopeless and pathetic-looking I knew you weren't a threat." She turned her fiery gaze to Rand. "This is obviously a trap!"

"I don't think so," Rand said, watching the man with something like interest. "He doesn't have the chill of the Dark One about him."

Lighting illuminated the beach, and for a brief moment they could see the man already fifty yards away. He looked over his shoulder and called to them, his voice surprisingly clear over the wind and waves. "Coming or not?"

"We don't have much better choice," Rand's eyes lingered on the stranger called Jack. "Just stay sharp. This is no ordinary man."

With a stream of obscenities from Joan they hurried up the muddy shore after him. Jack had been right; in less than twenty minutes they found themselves in another port town, half the size of Bale's Cove and twice as dilapidated. Barely more than a dozen shabby barnlike buildings stood at odd angles on the rocky beach, their walls and roofs patched with driftwood. The few ships docked on the single tiny pier creaked and rocked in the wind, their torn sails lashing like whips.

A sign simply marked INN hung above the only brick building's entrance, swinging almost horizontally against the wind. Light and laughter flickered through the dirty windows from within. Jack opened the door and strode inside, the place filled with laughing and shouting drunkards. The room was dominated by a large bar occupied by a motley assortment of patrons, clinking mugs and cracking jokes as they swayed on their stools.

Jack approached the bar, the others in tow, the heavyset barkeep eyeing him with suspicion through a haze of pungent pipe smoke. "What do you want?"

"I'm fine, thanks for asking. Are there any rooms available?"

A man at the bar leaned over, looking at Sam and the others with amusement. "Funny clothes you've got there," he pointed his mug towards Rand, Joan, and Thomas. "Lost your way from the circus?"

Several other patrons tittered. Joan and Rand gave the man glowering looks, while Thomas kept his eyes on the floor. Jack plucked at his soaked chin, still looking expectantly at the barman.

"We'll just be staying the one night. Long day of travelling, so if I could just have a key we'll be off to bed."

The barkeep looked around at their pale, clammy faces and took a pull off his pipe, stoking the bowl with his thumb. "We're full up."

"Are you sure about that?"

The man took another deep draw and blew a cloud of smoke into Jack's face. "I say we're full up, that means we're full up, so unless it's trouble you're after you and these brats better clear out of here."

70

Jack considered the red face through his matted hair, then reached into the breast of his jacket. For a moment the barkeep looked like he expected a knife to come out of the coat, when Jack reached forward and dropped a handful of gold coins on the greasy bar. The man choked on his smoke, coughing behind his fat fist as he gaped at the coins. One of the drunks at the bar spilled his flagon right down the front of his shirt.

Jack stood patient as the man caught his breath, the same expectant expression on his face. "What about now?"

The barkeep was staring at the coins as if he never knew such riches existed. After a moment he came to, stowed his pipe under the bar, then grinned and wringed his hands. "My sincerest apologizes, sir- ah, sirs- and-and miss, of course! We are pretty packed up tonight, what with the storm and all, but I think we can make special arrangements, just this once!"

He fumbled in his ill-fitting vest pockets and pulled out a key, which he held out to Jack with a trembling hand. "Straight up the stairs, first door on your right. Largest, most well-furnished room we have! It'll look a bit lived-in, being well, mine, but I can hardly send fine citizens of the world like yourselves out into a storm like this!"

"Appreciate it," Jack said, plucking they key from the barman's stubby fingers.

"Oh, my pleasure, sir, my pleasure!" The man's eyes were still on the gold. He produced an oil lamp from under the bar and singed his finger as he hurried to light it. "There are spare cots and blankets in the closet up there, plenty comfortable for your young charges. Is there anything else I can do for you, Mr.-?"

"As a matter of fact," Jack looked over the row of bottles behind the barkeep. "Have you got a decent bottle of brandy back there?"

The barkeep held up a forefinger and rummaged around under the bar. He pulled out a squat, dust-covered decanter and slid it across the bar. "Here we are, the finest stuff I have! Sorry about the dust, been aging it for years-"

"Shouldn't be a problem," Jack said, swiping up the bottle and reading the label. "Oh, and we're not to be disturbed. We've travelled far, and need our rest."

"Of course, sir! Wouldn't dream of it!"

Sam and the others followed Jack towards the staircase at the back of the room, as the barkeep scooped up the coins and jingled them with glee. "Enjoy your stay!" He called after them.

They climbed the narrow, creaking stairs, the barkeep's cheers of joy and the drunks' jealous groans fading beneath them. Guided by the lamp, Jack inserted the key into the first door on the right then poked his head and the lamp inside. "This'll do," he said, then disappeared into the darkened room. Sam and the others followed, letting the door close behind them.

Jack's silhouette crouched in front of a stone fireplace, and a moment later he had it burning bright. The warm light revealed a shabby but sizeable room filled with mismatched furniture. A large, lumpy bed sat beside a wardrobe with a missing door, a row of tattered clothing visible inside. An old desk stood in one corner, one of its spindly legs replaced with a stack of books.

"He paid all that gold for this?" Joan whispered. "That old goat probably would've given this dump up for one piece!"

"I'm not too worried about it," Joan jumped at Jack's words. He uncorked the bottle with his teeth and sniffed, his face pulling back with a wince. "Aging for years, eh? Aging what, exactly?" He took a swig and smacked his lips, nodding and holding the bottle to the light. "I stand corrected. Old buzzard knows his stuff."

He set the bottle on the bedside table, then kicked off his boots and placed them in front of the fire along with his overcoat. He warmed his hands for a moment before turning to the door by the bed, and began pulling folding cots from behind it.

"Sorry, I pay for the room, I get the bed." He handed one of the cots to Sam. "What's your name, kid?"

"Sam," he replied. The cot was for an adult, twice the size his at the Orphanage had been. "It's no problem, I'm used to sleeping in these."

"You're a lucky kid, then, Sam. Been sleeping in trees for the past month, myself. Sure, it's comfortable enough, but the bugs..."

He turned to Rand and held out a cot to him, but Rand didn't take it right away. He was surveying the man with a watchful, apprehensive look. "Who are you? What do you want with us?"

"Thought I told you, name's Jack, and at the moment I want you to cut the questions and take this damn cot."

He waited for Rand to take it, and after a tense moment he did. He handed the remaining cots to Joan and Thomas, who took them in silence. Jack twisted his beard in his fist and rang a stream of water from it, then took another swig from the bottle and began rummaging through the damaged wardrobe.

"Good thing our friend's a big boy," he said, examining a massive white nightshirt.

"Do you think you ought to be going through this man's belongings?" Rand said in disapproval.

"I doubt he'll mind, he's got enough gold to build a new inn if he likes." Jack removed his soaked shirt, his tan, wiry torso lined with tattoos. Emblems that looked something like a cross of a sword and a leaf adorned each arm, as did sharp, angular patterns on his shoulders and collarbones. He pulled the nightshirt over his head and tossed his own by the fire, then jumped into the bed and stretched.

"This isn't smart," Joan murmured to Rand as she and her brother unfolded their cots. "Storm or not we should be hiding, not cozied up at an inn."

"Feel free," Jack yawned, pointing toward the door with his eyes closed. Joan looked away and jabbed the fire with a poker. There was another long, contented yawn before Jack continued. "Now what's this bit about hiding?"

Rand fumed at Joan, who was now rearranging logs in the fire with her bare hands, avoiding the gaze of both of them. Jack sat upright, watching the four of them with a slight grin. "Well? What are you hiding from?"

"It's none of your concern," Rand said.

Jack's smile slackened. "I'm sorry to say that it's all of my concern. I think I have the right to know if I'm harboring a group of dangerous criminals, don't you?"

Rand didn't reply. Jack slicked his hair away from his eyes, his grey gaze intense, penetrating. "Maybe I'm just not asking the right question."

Joan's eyes narrowed. "What question?"

"You know damn well. What, exactly, were four young Strong doing in a backwater mortal pit like Bale's Cove?"

Sam looked from Rand to Joan, both of whom looked equally surprised. Thomas tore his eyes from the fire at the word and looked at his sister, terrified. Jack gave them a dangerous look, his glaring eyes moving from face to face. Sam could feel Rand and Joan tensing up on either side of him, ready to attack. Without warning, the man burst into a fit of laughter, throwing his head back and slapping his knee with delight.

Rand sprang forward, frost appearing on his fingertips. "Enough games! Who are you, and what you want with us? Tell me now!"

"Relax, there, slim," Jack said, still giggling between his words. "No need to get your hair in a twist."

Joan stepped beside Rand and looked at Jack with menace, grabbing him by the barkeep's shirt. "Tell us who you really are or you're joining those logs over there."

"Isn't it obvious? He's Strong too!"

Four heads cocked in Sam's direction. Rand and Joan looked mutinous, Thomas still terrified. Jack was no longer laughing. He batted Joan's hand away and looked at Sam with an expression that was difficult to read.

"What makes you say that?"

Sam watched the man, blue eyes on the grey. "The chain, the huge chain that was dragging me down. Part of it was still around my leg when I got into the lifeboat, the links at the end were squished like dough. There's no way any normal person could've broken that chain."

No one spoke. Sam and Jack contemplated one another, and finally, Jack's face cracked a grin. "You're a bright kid, Sam. Observant, resourceful, you keep a level head... you're the leader here, I take it?"

"Please," Joan spat, then rounded on Sam. "I know you're still new to this, Mr. Observant, but if he were Strong we'd know. We'd be able to feel it."

"Feel what? You mean this?"

It was instant, the warm prickling, in Sam's head and in his gut, the same feeling he'd felt when he first met Joan and Thomas. He'd grown numb to it after being with the others for days on end, but now it was surging again, the sharpness, the heightened sense of things, and he could tell from their faces that the others felt it too.

"You see?" Sam looked at the three of them. "I knew it!"

A moment later it subsided, as quickly as it appeared. Rand gaped at the man, looking alarmed, intrigued and envious all at once. "How did you do that?"

"Learned it back home. Old family secret, that sort of thing."

Joan looked nervously back from Jack to Rand, her eyes finally settling on Jack. "H-he is a Strong, then?"

"A Rogue," Rand said, looking at Jack with bitter under-standing. "It makes sense. No mortal could have done what he did back at sea."

"Don't sound so grateful, now," Jack said.

"What's a Rogue?" Sam asked.

"It's as simple as is sounds," Rand said, his eyes still on Jack. "Rogues are Strong who left their homes and their lives behind. An extreme act for one of our kind, for once one does so they are never welcomed back."

"Why did you leave?" Sam asked Jack.

"Typically, Strong leave their kingdoms for two reasons," Rand answered for him, his eyes cold. "Exile for a high crime, or a hunger for power and conquest."

"Is that right?" Jack said. "Which are you out here for, then? Correct me if I'm wrong, but the four of you are quite a ways from any kingdom I'm aware of."

"You're the only Rogue here," Joan said, her tone com-bative. "And no matter what the reason they left Rogues can never be trusted."

Jack frowned. "I've saved your scrawny hides, paid room and board for the evening, and you've returned the favor with false accusations and threats? Seems to me you're the ones that can't be trusted in this room."

"He does have a point," Sam said, a tinge of guilt in his words. "We're sorry."

"Sorry? *Sorry?*" Joan looked furious, almost frantic. "You fool- how do we know he's not waiting for us to fall asleep so he can cut our throats?"

"There's an interesting theory," Jack chuckled. "Paranoid and delusional, but definitely interesting. Make a good storybook tale, that would."

He got to his feet and squared his shoulders. "Here's a dif-ferent theory for you, girlie. If I wanted you dead, don't you think I could have saved myself quite a bit of grief by leaving you on the boat? And kids or not, there's four of you and only one of me, so it was me taking the real risk approaching you, was it not?"

"Why were you following us in the first place?" Rand demanded. "You were... concealed or however you call it, you could've passed us by and we would've been none the wiser."

"Well, it's not every day you run into another Strong, now is it? You can imagine my curiosity when I saw the four of you stumbling around those rat-infested docks."

Jack surveyed them with a knowing look. "I should've expected this sort of reaction. I could spot the fear in you a mile away."

"Fear of what, exactly?" Rand asked.

"I've asked you that twice, and I still haven't gotten an answer."

It was Sam who finally spoke after him. "I understand how you guys feel, but he's helped us so much already," Sam went on despite Rand and the siblings' wary faces. "And Rand, you said yourself you didn't think he's one of the necro-"

Joan clapped her hand over his mouth with an echoing slap. Jack jumped right in front of Sam, his grey eyes wide and intense. "What did you just say?"

"Nothing," Joan snapped. "He doesn't know what he's-"

Jack held up a hand for silence, which Joan surprisingly obeyed. Sam shrugged her off and turned back to Jack, and thought he saw fear in the hair covered face.

"Did you say... did you say necromancer?"

Rand and Joan gave him warning looks, but Sam answered anyway. "Yes."

Jack hesitated for a moment, looking stricken. "You...you know about him?"

"We do."

Sam kept his answers short, unsure how the man was going to react. It was always easier to hide fear back in the alleys if the bullies couldn't hear the quiver in your voice. He wasn't exactly afraid at the moment, though. Judging by the look on his face, it seemed like Jack would sooner leap out the window in fright than try to harm them. The man made no response, so Sam decided it was his turn to proceed. "So... you know about him, too, then?"

Jack stepped back, frightened comprehension growing under the beard. He grabbed the bottle and crossed to the fireplace, then sunk into a chair beside it with a haunted expression.

"A few months back I was exploring a ruin to the west called the Citadel of Souls. It's an ancient tower that holds the tombs of some of the greatest of our kind. I'd been there a few hours when I felt something, a burning kind of like what Strong feel when we're around each other. I hadn't seen another one of us in years, I wanted to meet them when it... when it came over me."

"When what came over you?" Sam asked.

"It's hard to describe. I felt cold first, cold inside, nothing to do with weather. Dread started to fill me, dread that hurt like real pain. I started forgetting things, like my mind was going blank, and the cold, the cold and dread doubled every second. I couldn't see, I couldn't feel... it was like I was being... drained from myself."

He paused for a swig of brandy. "I heard footsteps, hundreds of footsteps coming closer and closer. I was losing my mind, losing myself... but a fleeting memory passed through my head, and somehow I was able to conceal myself. The pain stopped instantly. Everything flooded back to me, my memories, my strength, but I could still feel that cold inside me. I still feel it sometimes."

"I heard voices and ran, ran as fast as I could, and hid in the tallest tree I could find. Men came walking beneath me, scores of men in black armor. A tall man with a hood led them, and the moment I saw him I felt the chill again. I concentrated all my strength on concealing myself, and thank the stars they passed without finding me. And then..."

"The tall man stretched out his hands, and dark clouds rolled in, lightning started crashing, and...and people started walking out of the Citadel, dressed in armor, holding weapons, only they weren't people, they... they were dead. Hundreds of dead Strong were marching out of the tower towards him. That's when I realized the men in black armor... they were all dead, too."

Rand and Joan exchanged looks. Jack shuddered before speaking again. "They assembled at the entrance in front of this guy, and they...they bowed before him. I...I thought they were gone, I couldn't believe it what I was seeing, it... it was one of the Dark Ones."

They were all staring at him, wide-eyed and silent. Jack looked haunted as he stared back at them, shaking from head to foot. "He's looking for you... isn't he?"

Sam spoke after a chilling pause. "Yes. He is."

"Listen, you kids have got to move," Jack got to his feet and began pacing around the room. "If he already has those things out this way they're bound to catch up with you. You've put a good distance between you by boat, but if you get too close to them they'll be able to feel your power. I can keep you covered there for now, but-"

"Wait a minute," Rand interrupted. "Are you saying you can conceal others as well as yourself?"

"You catch on quick. It's going to take some getting used to, I usually don't keep much company, but it seems to be working well enough so far. I've been hiding the five of us since the ship boarded and no skeletons breaking down the door yet, right?"

Jack cracked a smile, but none of them returned it. He took another drink and cleared his throat. "You'll be safe here for the night. Come daybreak I can help you find a place to hide."

"Hide?" Sam said.

79

"I know a spot in the mountains not too far from here, we could be there in two days' time if we don't make any stops. There's clean water and game to hunt in the area, you could stay there for as long as you needed to."

"What if we run into more skeletons?" Joan asked. "You didn't sound very confident about hiding all five of us."

"No one's going to find *me*. Where I come from, stealth is second nature."

"Of course!" Sam exclaimed. "You're one of the Sharpwood warriors!"

Jack looked alarmed, almost embarrassed, but recovered himself quickly. "Where did you hear that name?"

"In here!"

Sam pulled out the book and handed it to Jack, flipping to the designated page for him. "There's a whole story in here, a tribe of swordsmen specializing in stealth and concealment."

Jack skimmed the page then began thumbing through the rest of the book, his eyes almost popping out of his head. "Where on earth did you get this?"

"My parents left it to me," He looked away from the dumbfounded man and turned excitedly to the others. "He can help us!"

Jack looked confused. "Help you what?"

"We're trying to find the other Strong, and warn them that these monsters coming for them. We're going to stop this necromancer before he kills them all!"

Jack laughed. "Kid, what you expect to do? I admire the initiative and all, but this is way beyond the four of you."

"Well, the four of us maybe, but if we can convince the Strong join forces, we might be able to-"

"Look, I've tangled with this guy before. He nearly killed me without even seeing me. Besides, Strong don't like outsiders, you ought to know that by now. Even if you make it to one of the kingdoms they'll never trust you."

"Well," Sam looked hopeful. "What if we had a member of the kingdom with us?"

Jack laughed again. "I should've seen that coming. Forget it."

"But don't you see? If you don't help us, your home is going to be destroyed!"

"I'm already over it," Jack said.

"It doesn't matter," Rand said, stepping in front of Sam and staring Jack in the face. "We don't need him. We have the maps and our instincts to guide us."

Jack shook his head. "Those better be some damn good maps."

"I'm going to sleep," Rand snapped, turning away from Jack toward the others. "And you all should do the same. We have a long road ahead of us."

With one last glare at Jack he crossed the room to his cot and settled into it. Jack drained the rest of the brandy, staring at the empty bottle with his brow furrowed. Sam looked beseechingly at Joan, who only shrugged and turned to her own cot. Sam looked back to Jack, who had begun scratching at label on the bottle.

"Please, we-"

"Kid, you've got heart, that I can see, but there's nothing you or anyone can do to stop this. The only thing you can do is get as far out of the way as you can."

"We have to try. You know the way back to your home, I know you do. Please, show us the way."

"It's not that simple. Even if I wanted to, it would mean crossing through-"

"Sharpwood Forest," Jack looked surprised at Sam's answer. "We know the risks, we were prepared to face them before we ran into you, and we'd be even more prepared having you with us."

"Prepared?" Jack gave him a serious look. "I've been watching you four since the cove. You barely get along amongst yourselves, let alone with anyone else. How do you expect to convince a kingdom to trust you when you don't even trust each other?"

"You gave us a chance, maybe they will, too." Sam squeezed the book in his hands. "Please, we need your help."

Jack looked down at the floor, and let the bottle drop from his hand. It rolled across the floor and out of sight, into the shadows beneath the bed. He heaved a deep sigh and looked back up at Sam, looking grim. "I'll lead you through the forest to the outskirts of the kingdom, but that's as far as I go. I swore I'd never go back after I left, and I meant it."

Sam could have jumped for joy. "Thank you so much, I-"

"Just get some rest. Like Ponytail over there said, it's a long road ahead, and this'll likely going to be the last night you sleep in a cot for a long time."

Sam nodded and climbed into the remaining cot. The full sized cot was sturdy and tear-free, feeling to Sam like a bed fit for a king. Jack moved his seat in front of the fire and began jabbing it with a poker. A few cots over Sam heard Rand scoffing under his breath: "Ponytail, humph. Classless barbarian."

# VIII

The sound of creaking cots and the familiar sagging of one beneath him jolted Sam from his sleep like a splash of ice water. He shot upright and glanced around, and thanked the heavens when he saw that he'd woken up at the inn and not the Orphanage. He stretched and went to stand when a mass of fabric was thrown over his head. As he pulled it off he realized it was his own coat, now dry from the night in front of the fireplace.

"I was just about to wake you," Joan's agitated voice came from behind him. "Move it, it's already past daybreak."

Sam pulled the coat off and saw her and the others up and about buckling boots or fastening buttons. The newest member of the group was nowhere to be seen, the empty bottle by the closet door the only sign of him.

"Where's Jack?" Sam asked.

"He was already gone when I woke," Rand said. "He must have done his little trick again; I didn't hear a sound all night. Fortunately, he didn't take this." He picked up the book from the bedside table and handed it to Sam. Sam took it and held it in his lap, giving the pages a forlorn flip.

"He's gone?"

"Good riddance," Joan said as she helped her brother fasten a buckle on his shoulder. "We didn't need him, anyway."

Sam walked to the window. The sky was pink over the vast green sea, its waters calm as they gently washed against the shore. Gulls screeched they scanned the beach for food. Masts poked into view a short distance away, their ravaged sails being already replaced by their crewmen. He looked down to the street and saw a handful of people walking about the small village, but Jack wasn't one of them.

"I can't believe he left..."

"I told you Rogues couldn't be trusted," Joan finished buckling her boots and straightened up. "Let's get out of here quick, we don't need that smokestack of a barman downstairs asking any questions."

Sam put on his hat and glanced around for his shoes, when it occurred to him he'd lost one the night before. The other was missing too now, its muddy footprint left on the floor by his cot. He looked around for it when the door swung open and someone came striding in, a burlap sack in their hands.

"About time," Jack said, opening the sack and rummaging through it. "I thought you'd all died in your sleep."

Rand looked disappointed at the man's return. "And where were you?"

"Someone needed to prepare while you four were snoozing."

"Prepare for what?" Joan asked.

"He's agreed to help us," Sam answered, his eagerness returning. "He's going to show us the way to the forest!"

"Is that so?" Rand said, giving Jack a measuring look. "Why the change of heart?"

"Call it a moral dilemma. If I left here knowing I'd sent four helpless, dim-witted kids to their doom I could never live with myself." He pulled clothes from the sack and tossed them to Rand, Joan, and Thomas. "Put these on, that foreign garb of yours attracts too much attention. Let's go, we haven't got all day!"

The three of them did as they were told and pulled the clothes over their own. Jack produced a pair of brown leather boots from the sack and handed them to Sam. "Give these a try, did my best to match the size with your old one."

"Those were too big to begin with," Sam said, taking the boots and pulling them on. They were still a bit large for him but fit better than his old shoes, the sides stiff and sturdy, the soles warm and plush. "Thanks."

"You'll grow into them. Now hurry it up, we need to get a move on!"

When they'd finished Joan was dressed in a simple white shirt and a pair of faded trousers, her brother in a moth-eaten jacket and pants that made him look like a red-headed Sam. Rand wore stained brown slacks and a dark shirt covered in small burns, several of its tarnished buttons missing.

"Perfect," Jack said as he took in their shabby appearances. "Plain and pathetic as any yokel in this run-down port, now let's get out of here."

Jack locked the room behind them and they headed downstairs, where some of the inn's guests were already stirring. A man in pajamas was reading by one of the windows, sipping from a steaming mug. An old woman fiddled with a knot as she sat knitting by the fireplace. Several sailors were already pounding drinks at the bar, exchanging tales of their time at sea.

"Good morning!" A voice called, and Sam noticed the innkeeper polishing a coin by the bar. His eyes were heavy and bloodshot, but he looked as jovial as he had when he first laid eyes on the gold. "Had a comfortable night, I trust?"

The coin dropped into his jingling vest pocket, his grin straining his fat cheeks. "Hungry? I can fix you all a breakfast fit for a king! Eggs, bacon, sausage, anything you like! What'll it be?"

"Thank you, but we must be on our way," Jack said. He pulled the room key from his pocket and handed it back to the barkeep.

Sam's stomach snarled at the thought of a real meal. "Couldn't we just-"

"We need to get going," Jack said in a stern voice, then put out a hand to the barkeep. "We appreciate the hospitality."

"My pleasure, sir!" He grasped Jack's hand in both of his own and shook, Jack's other arm giving an involuntary twitch. "If you're ever passing through again, be sure to look us up! Have a safe journey, now!"

Outside the sandy roadways were strewn with debris, the inhabitants of the village cleaning up the aftermath of the storm. Carts and wheelbarrows were loaded with trash while others tried to repair the damage to their property. A barn across from the inn had collapsed, the heavy broken beams piled like matchsticks. A group of burly men were worked by the shore dragging chunks of debris from the beach.

Two of them carried a large hunk of wood past Sam and the others, and Sam saw the wistful face of the figurehead from their ship. One of her eyes had been gouged away, the remaining one looking at him as if a tear may stream from the wood. In all the terror and chaos of the previous night he hadn't given much thought to the ship's other passengers. Only now did it occur to him there was no way any of them could have survived.

A toothless hag pushing along a wheelbarrow stopped and spoke to them. "Yes, yes, dreadful thing, more than two dozen went down with her, the way I heard it."

Four men used ropes to haul a section of the ship's hull up the beach, followed by another group muscling a portion of the mast. The old woman watched them pass, shaking her head in dismay. "That bloody storm came out of nowhere, the poor souls didn't stand a chance."

"Better them than us," Jack said, indifferent as he continued moving. With a scowl she was off, the wheel in front of her squeaking in the sand.

"Hey! You!"

The five of them turned to see three men running towards them from the direction of the inn, dressed only in their underpants. People stared as they raced down the street, shaking fists at Sam and the others.

"My clothes!" One of the men shouted. "You get back here!"

"They've robbed me, too!" A heavier man was huffing after the three of them, a pipe clenched in his teeth. "They've stolen my hard-earned gold! Stop those thieves!"

"Time to go," Jack said, sprinting up the beach.

Sam and the others dashed after him as more villagers joined the barkeep and the other men. They raced out of the tiny town and up the coast, outrunning their pursuers easier than Sam would've ever thought. He'd never run so fast in his life, leaving a trail of long boot prints in the sand at the other's heels. They didn't stop for more than a mile, turning away from the shore and coming to rest at a small rock outcropping by the edge of the sands.

"Looks like we lost them," Jack said when he regained his breath.

"You stole these?" Rand panted, tugging at the filthy shirt he wore.

"What choice did I have?" Jack sounded as innocent as a man of the cloth. "I spent all my gold on the room."

"You stole that back, too!" Joan exclaimed.

"And now we have both the gold and the clothes. Win-win, don't you think?"

Rand hopped onto a tall rock and scanned for any sign of followers. Satisfied, he leapt down and landed face to face with Jack, looking at the bearded man with disdain. "Are you expecting us to trust our lives to a common thief?"

"No, I'm expecting you to trust me." Jack regarded the young man. "We don't have to like each other, but if we're going to proceed from here the least we can do is trust each other."

He held out his hand to Rand. The young man stared down his nose at it, then reached out and gave a single shake. "Well, lead the way," Rand said, releasing his grip at once. "I don't want to lose our head start."

They followed Jack east, away from the sea and over a stretch of rocky hills. He proved to be a great navigator and an even better tracker. Each night he caught wild hares or birds, or found heaps of berries and edible roots for them to eat. Sam had never eaten so well in his life. Rand made every attempt to outperform Jack on hunts, but each night the man brought back a bigger hare, a fatter pheasant or wild turkey, always accompanied by the same wild-eyed grin.

"I've been wondering," Sam asked him as they camped by a river's edge one night, eating fish Jack had caught by hand. "Why did you leave home?"

"It's complicated," Jack picked his teeth with a fishbone.

"Likely stealing gold in the dead of night," Rand muttered under his breath.

"For your information, I didn't take it in the dead of night. I snatched it back just as we were leaving the inn."

"I thought I saw you move," Sam said, sounding almost impressed. "You grabbed it while he was shaking your hand, didn't you?"

"Good eye kid," Jack gave a mischievous smile. "I've been using those same coins for years. Mortals as so easy to trick."

"Obviously not, he noticed a minute later," Joan said. "I'd bet a whole pile of gold the other Strong kicked you out."

"Let me put it this way. It was either leave or die, and it wasn't hard to decide."

"What happened?" Rand asked.

"Politics," Jack said in a vague voice.

Sam's brows contracted. "Politics?"

"There was a...*shift* in the tribal leadership, and I felt compelled to leave."

Joan was looking interested. "What kind of shift?"

"It's getting late," Jack got to his feet with a yawn. "A few more days and we'll reach the edge of the forest. From there things get a lot trickier."

He kicked dirt over the fire and walked off, settling himself against a nearby tree without another word. They all did the same, each finding a dry spot to sleep. Sam stayed awake for another hour or so, laying in the grass and staring at the stars. The moon was bright above him, its light floating on the river's rippling surface.

He felt nervous about the days to come. He'd read the book enough times to know just how dangerous a trip into the Sharpwood Forest was going to be. Having Jack with them did lighten his fears about the journey, but there was also the matter of meeting the Strong as well. The kingdoms didn't welcome outsiders, and Sam had no idea how the people would react to a band of 'Rogues'.

He thought about what Jack had said the night they met him. *How do you expect to convince a kingdom to trust you when you don't even trust each other?* Bicker and argue as they might, Sam could say that he trusted Rand, Joan and Thomas. They must have trusted him to some degree or they never would have agreed to the journey in the first place, certainly more than they trusted Jack. To say their relationship was strained was an understatement, but they were closest thing Sam ever had to friends.

He supposed it didn't make much difference as he drifted off to sleep. With so much hanging in the balance, what did trusting each other really matter? They had to warn the Sharpwood warriors, and all the other Strong or the necromancer's monsters would destroy them. Once they heard what the four of them had to say, there was no way the people of the forest wouldn't believe them.

The five of them continued east, still seeing no signs of Bones or his undead army. Sam hoped that Rand had been right, and that the horde of monsters was still days behind them. After nearly a week of treading rocky plains and dark woods they saw a tall cliff in the distance, its cracked red face matching the sky as the sun began to set.

"The Red Ridge," Jack said as they approached the barren red wall. "At the top we'll find the outskirts of the forest, and the edge of the mortal world."

Sam looked up the nearly vertical rock face. "We're climbing this?"

"The Sharpwood warriors hid their home well," Jack said. "It's what they do, after all."

"What's the matter?" Joan taunted. "Afraid of heights?"

"It's not as bad as it looks," Jack gave Sam a reassuring look. "I wasn't all that much older than you when I did it."

"Let's just get to it," Rand said, grasping the rocky wall and starting to climb. "We need to reach the summit while we still have sunlight."

They began their precarious climb, moving inch by inch up the dusty red rock. Jack was in the lead, his hands and feet propelling him up the side of the cliff with ease. Rand was close behind while Joan climbed at an even pace with a nervous-looking Thomas. Sam brought up the rear as always, kicking his new boots into the rock to hold himself steady.

"Are you sure this is the only way?" Joan called to Jack above her. "No stairs, anything?"

"Afraid not," Jack yelled back. "I thought it'd it be clear by now the place is supposed to be difficult to reach."

About halfway up the rock began to steepen, and hand and footholds were becoming fewer and farther between. Sam's fingers were turning raw as he grunted and panted behind the others. He kept his eyes forward, unwilling to even imagine how high up he was at this point. There was still quite a way to go, and the top of the cliff seemed as out of reach as the sky itself.

Sam stretched up for a protruding rock but released it when it shifted slightly at his touch. There was nothing else to grab hold to, so he wiggled it back and forth to test its strength. It didn't budge this time, feeling firm as a mortared brick. He grabbed hold of it and carefully pulled himself up, reaching out and digging his outstretched fingers into another groove above it. Hoisting himself up, he placed his foot on the rock and reached up for the next, when the stone slid and gave out under his weight.

With a cry of shock he slid down the face of the cliff, scraping his chest and face against the rough rock. He flailed his arms forward to try to stop himself but there was nowhere on the flat wall for him to grip. Desperately he clawed at the rock, red dust spraying his eyes and mouth. Fragments of rock bounced off the top of his hat as he felt himself somehow slowing down, his legs dangling as his fingers held on.

Jack had climbed down to help but stopped, hanging a few yards above him in amazement. Through the dust Sam could see his fingers, sticking into the solid rock as if it were clay. Long score marks were carved into the cliff leading down to where he hung. With a grin he reached up and dug his fingers in, the rock giving way to his grip with little effort.

Up he went, passing all four of them as if climbing a ladder. Once he reached the top he flopped onto the grass to catch his breath. Minutes later he heard the others growing closer and looked down to help them. He reached out a hand to Rand which he refused, the pale young man climbing up and dusting himself off in a dignified manner. Joan and Thomas followed, then Jack, who laughed as he rolled onto the clifftop.

"Nice save," he said, clapping Sam on the back as he walked by.

"It was luck," Joan said as she brushed red dust from her clothes. "Nothing but dumb luck." She turned to Jack. "Now where do we-"

Jack wandered away, looking down the valley beyond the cliff. At the bottom was the start of a vast, dense forest, stretching out as far as the eye could see under the setting sun. It was clear even from this distance that the trees were massive, likely hundreds, even thousands of years old.

He stood looking over the valley in silence, then cleared his throat then turned to the others. "We'll camp here until morning. Make sure you get some rest, sleeping in here is going to be tough."

"Sleep?" Joan said. "How long is this going to take?"

"It's two days through the forest to the village. Like I said,-"

"Yeah, yeah, well-hidden, it's what you do, we know, we know. Thomas, help me gather some wood, we'll get a fire going."

# IX

They woke early the next morning, the massive trees at the forest's border waiting like a line of gargantuan soliders. Sam marveled at their height, stretching a hundred feet into the blue sky above. He couldn't explain it but he felt an energy from them, like the great timbers were watching, contemplating the five tiny strangers at their roots. Jack was already looking through them, his eyes tense, focused like a predator on the hunt.

"Everyone stay close and keep your eyes all around you. This isn't going to be your average walk in the woods."

He stepped into the trees and the others slowly followed, the morning sun obscured almost at once by the thick canopy. The humid air smelled clean and sweet; Sam was reminded of a slice of apple pie that Miss Sarah had given him one summer. The pleasant scent did little to quell the fear coiling in his stomach as he spun at every creaking branch, every sound of movement from the endless brush surrounding them.

"Fascinating," Rand was standing on a boulder after they'd covered a few miles, examining a vine covered in flamboyant purple and yellow petals. "I've never seen so many different plant species."

"There mustn't be much up where you're from," Jack said.

"That's why I find them so intriguing," Rand looked at the bark of the tree the vine hung from, its upper branches disappearing into the dense foliage above. "This must have been an interesting place to grow up."

"Interesting's certainly one way to put it, now let's keep a move on. There'll be plenty of time to smell the flowers when you get to the village."

Rand hopped down and followed behind the others. A faint rustling brushed behind him, and as he turned his eyes went wide with shock. The flowered vine he'd been admiring moments before now stood arched above him like a serpent, the bright petals curled into dripping, pointed spines. Rand had barely a moment to react before it lashed, circling him in a whirl of colored spikes.

Wind rushed and frost flew as he conjured a ball of snowy wind around himself. The vine recoiled at the cold and Rand thrust out his palms, spraying the ice right over it. It froze in place for a moment before toppling, shattering on the ground like an ice sculpture. Rand panted as he looked down at the frozen shards of plant matter, his face pink and sweating.

"What was that?"

"Razorvine," Jack sounded casual as ever. "The purple and yellow petals are a dead giveaway."

"You knew?" Rand looked livid. "Why didn't you say anything?"

"Just making sure you're keeping on your toes. For my own safety, you understand."

Jack jumped onto a mossy clutch of roots, slicking hair from his eyes to clear his view. With another leap he grabbed a low-hanging branch and swung upward, seizing another and launching higher. He hoisted himself up, fifty feet above them, holding the tree for balance. After a moment he leapt back down, grabbing a thin, flowerless vine and swinging right to them.

"We're going to see worse than thorny vines before this little adventure is over. If we're going to make it through here in one piece we're going to need to find weapons."

"We have no need for weapons," Rand said with a tip of his nose. "Haven't I just proved that?"

"For once we agree," Joan crossed her arms, looking at her brother. "We don't need sticks and stones to handle ourselves."

"Just wait, once you see you're going to want one of these sticks."

Jack leapt back into the trees and took off into the foliage. The others hurried after him, Rand determined to follow close. Jack paused here and there, scanning the ground beneath him before jumping off again. After a while he must have seen what he was looking for, and Sam saw him drop to the forest floor.

They found him standing next to a tall spiked mass, what looked like a bush comprised of flat, pointed thorns each between two and three feet in length. Jack walked around it examining the thorns, squinting at the spaces between them.

"Is that what I think it is?" Sam asked.

"What is it?" Joan looked wary as Jack extended a careful hand and reached toward the center of the bush. With a snap he pulled one free and looked it over from end to end. Jack turned the thorn in his hands, holding it lengthwise and staring down the tip. Its two sharp edges led to a grooved green root, which Jack grasped like the hilt of a sword.

Rand gave him an impatient look as the man passed the thorn back and forth in his hands. "You do whatever makes you feel safer, but I don't need-"

There was a swish and a rush of wind as Jack slashed the thorn against a nearby tree. It left no mark, but a moment later the tree slipped in half, the green rings within glistening with sap. He swung the blade in a flurry of intricate strokes before coming to an abrupt stop with the blade held in front of his eyes.

"Good weight, nice balance, root's not too thick..." He turned back to Rand, who was still gaping at the hewn tree. "Well? Waiting for an invitation?"

95

Rand shook off his bewilderment and reached between the swordlike leaves, struggling for a few moments before prying one free. He held the thorn out with his right hand and gave it a few quick swings as Jack turned to the siblings. "Next."

Joan reached both hands into the bush and grabbed one for her and her brother, but Thomas was already tugging one of his own. After some straining each of them pulled out a blade, then Jack nodded to Sam. "You're up."

Sam hesitated. "Are you sure this is safe?"

The look on Jack's face was answer enough. Sam reached for the root of one about the length of his arm, took careful hold and pulled, but the thorn held firmly in place.

"Give it a little twist as your pulling," Jack said. "Should pop right out."

Sam did as he was told, but it still wouldn't budge. He grabbed with both hands and finally yanked it out, falling backward onto the ground once it popped loose. He could hear Joan laughing as he got up, his eyes still on the mass of thorns. Jack shifted his attention back to the forest. "We're a bit off track, but if we bear south we can-"

Sam backed away as the bush began to shake, the thorns quivering as if they'd somehow frightened the plant. Jack noticed and he too looked alarmed, his grey eyes wide with surprise.

"Run!"

They fled in a panicked scramble as the bush thrashed harder and faster, then with an echoing snap the thorns fired off in every direction like a hail of spears. Sam dove behind a tree as the barrage whizzed past, the tree shuddering as thorn after thorn sunk into its trunk. He felt a tap as the tip of one pierced the bark, poking a hole in his coat pocket but thankfully missing his hip.

When the swishing and thudding stopped he peered around the tree for the others. Just about every tree he saw was spiked with thorns, some of them still quivering from impact. Rand's head poked out from behind one of them, looking stricken. Joan's popped out from around another, followed by the milk-white face of her brother. Jack dropped from a branch above, looking at a round, rocklike object sitting in the bushes' place, pockmarked with holes like a hunk of cheese.

"That was close," he panted, looking at Sam. "How did you know it was going to blow?"

"The thorn's roots were green. The book says that if the root's still green, the spines haven't fully hardened in place."

Jack laughed and slapped his shoulder, making Sam's knees buckle. "I should've noticed that myself. Guess I've been away a little too long."

"Guess so," Joan said, looking at a severed lock of her own hair pinned to a nearby tree.

On they went, twice running into more razorvines, their new weapons making quick work of the monstrous plants. Sam was amazed by the blade's light weight and strength; it felt like slicing through the Foundry's hardest steel with Agatha's switch. Joan and Thomas were making equal use of both the thorns and their flames, while Rand relied more heavily on his command of the cold.

Sam's power was no longer fleeting, but fully with him as he fought the forest's dangers. His movements were fast and fluid, his sense of his surroundings was almost supernatural. He felt himself able to anticipate attacks, bringing his weapon to block before the strike was even coming. The vines fell in twitching tangles as he tore through them, more than once saving each of the others from one they missed.

When night began to fall Jack led them up a tall tree draped in dense clumps of vines. The brown, flower-free ropes were tough and strong, and Jack showed them how to make quick, sturdy hammocks using only a few of them. While they worked he slung the one he fashioned for himself over his shoulder and climbed the vine drenched branches. He set his hammock up high above where they tied theirs, keeping watch with his thorn in his lap.

Sam lay awake while the others slept on either side of him, Joan snoring in his ear through her tangled hair. He watched Jack sitting above, his shaggy head slowly turning like a large grizzled owl. He knew Rand and Joan couldn't wait to be rid of him, probably Thomas as well, but Sam had come to consider Jack a real part of their makeshift group. Aside from Miss Sarah he was the only person who'd ever helped him with anything, and for that he had Sam's gratitude and respect.

It occurred to him how little he knew about the man above him, to whom he already owed so much. In the weeks since he'd joined them Jack had said nothing about his past, changing or avoiding the subject whenever it came up. Abandoning the prospect of sleep, Sam hopped out of his hammock, grabbed a vine and began to climb. He saw Jack's head poke out above him as he got closer, the grey eyes narrowed behind the mass of hair.

"I thought I told you to get some sleep," Jack's voice was hushed but stern as Sam grew level with his hammock.

"I can't," The tree's limbs creaked as Sam pulled himself onto a branch beside him.

"Keep it down!" Jack cocked his head from side to side, his thorn tight in his fist. "The girl's snoring is bad enough."

"Sorry," Sam looked around for any sign of danger. "Do you think something will find us?"

Jack continued to scan the surrounding branches. "Probably not," He admitted after a moment. "This is a quieter area, that's why we stopped here... but still, there's no place in this forest I'd want to let my guard down."

"You still remember your way around this place pretty well, huh?"

"Like the back of my hand," Jack said. "This tree was a favorite spot of mine as a kid."

Sam looked in the direction Jack was facing and immediately saw why. The tree they sat in grew at the edge of a cliff, overlooking a wide expanse of forest that stretched out like a rolling green ocean before them. The night sky was bright with thousands of stars, the infinite lights blinking and winking at him across the eons in a twinkling, shimmering cloud. Sam had never seen so many, their light glowing on his face after travelling lifetimes to greet him.

"Wow."

"I thought the same thing first time I saw it," Jack watched the sky with a musing, almost wistful face. "Sure makes you feel small, staring at something so big. Now go on, you need to get some rest."

"I'm too excited to sleep," Starlight reflected the eagerness in Sam's eyes. "Tomorrow I'm actually going to see the one of the kingdoms of the Strong!"

"Don't get too excited," Jack said. "It's not going to be the fairytale land your little storybook would have you think. Remember, the village hasn't had a visitor in centuries, they have no use for the outside world. I highly doubt there'll be a parade in your honor when you show up."

Sam was still optimistic. "Maybe not, but once they hear what we have to tell them, I'm sure they'll help us."

You'd better hope," Jack turned his attention from the forest to Sam. "So... The long-haired kid said you were raised by mortals. What's the story there?"

"There's not much to tell, I guess. I never knew my family, I was left at an orphanage when I was a baby. They found me in a basket on the front steps, along with this," He patted his chest where the book was stowed. "That's all that I know."

"I've heard of our kind living with mortals before, but never being raised by them," Jack was looking thoughtfully at him. "Rogues will try to slip among them and keep their powers secret, but it's always a matter of time before they slip up and someone no-

99

tices. That's why I never stay in one place for too long. In all that time at that orphanage no one ever noticed anything... different about you?"

"They noticed, alright," Sam's words were bitter. "The way I healed made everyone pick on me twice as bad. It was like a contest to see who could leave a lasting mark."

"Damn," Jack said. "Don't those sorts of places have, you know, supervision?"

Sam scoffed. "The old hags who ran the place turned a blind eye to all of it. They thought I was a freak, too. The headmistress used to joke she'd sell me to the circus if it ever came to town."

"Not a bad idea," Jack stroked his beard. "I mean, from their point of view, of course," he clarified as Sam frowned. "Sounds like you had it pretty tough growing up. Think I would've taken my chances out here over all that."

"Now maybe you understand why I'm happy to be doing this," Sam said.

"You remind me a lot of myself as a kid. I couldn't wait to get away from home, either."

"I can't see why," Sam looked back to the stars. "This is the most beautiful place I've ever seen."

"It is beautiful," Jack allowed. "As scary as things can be out here, you can really find peace at times. I felt more at home here in the wild than I ever did in the village."

"What's it like?" Sam tried to keep his voice down in spite of his excitement. "The kingdom, I mean. What are the people like?"

"Above all else, boring," Jack prodded at the tree with his thorn. "Life in the village is all about tradition, living by the sacred teachings of the ancients." His voice dripped with sarcasm. "Bunch of silly superstition, if you ask me. Who wants to wake up every morning at the crack of dawn to pray to the roots and bugs, or fast for a week if it didn't rain on some particular Friday? They had a rule for everything, and if you broke even one you wouldn't hear the end of it."

"When we weren't practicing some foolish ritual or back-breaking training, we learned about our people's history from the village elders. That wasn't so bad. We would gather in the village square and they would tell stories of our ancestors, how they built our home, the battles they fought against invaders from beyond the forest. I always pictured myself as the one saving the kingdom, fighting off bad guys from the outside world."

He made a playful flourish with his sword, imitating a duel with an imaginary foe. Sam smiled inwardly; until only a few weeks ago, he'd been doing the same thing every night with the stories in his book.

"The outside world," Jack repeated, the wildness in his eyes returning in the starlight. "It was an obsession of mine for as long as I can remember. There was more out there beyond those trees, waiting for me if I could only get to it. I think I was about nine the first time I tried sneaking into the forest on my own... Heh, I didn't make it more than a mile before running scared back to the village."

"By yourself?" Sam always had a thirst for adventure growing up, but somehow he couldn't imagine his nine-year-old self being nearly as brave as that. "Shouldn't you have brought a few friends to watch your back?"

"Didn't have many, truth be told. I never got on well with other kids my age. All any of them wanted to do was carry on their family legacy, be a proud Sharpwood warrior like their father, and his father, and his father, you get the idea. They were all content to live and die here, never even wondering what else is out there."

"As I got older I got braver, after I'd learned a few tricks with a thorn, and before long I knew my way around here as well as I did the village. By the time I was sixteen I'd probably seen more of the forest on my own than most of the village elders. It used to piss my father off something awful. After a while he started sending guards to find me and bring me back."

"Your father had guards?" Sam asked. "He must've been someone important."

"He sure thought so," Jack continued to dig at the bark. "He worked in the palace, for the royal family of the kingdom. It was the greatest thing in the world to him, living out the same life as everyone in his line before him. All he ever wanted was for me to follow in his footsteps, to continue the family legacy after he was gone. I hated the idea. I didn't want to live a life I was born into, I wanted to make my own destiny."

"It doesn't sound so bad," Sam considered. "Growing up in a palace sounds like it must've been something!"

Jack snorted.

"It might have been a palace to some, but to me it was a prison. Service to the kingdom meant wasting away inside its borders, trapped forever while the world passed me by. Just the thought of it pushed me deeper and deeper into the forest. I remember the first time I made it all the way through... standing at the edge of the Red Ridge, the horizon that went on forever... once I saw that endless blue sky, I just had to see everything beneath it."

"That little trip earned me quite a bit of grief. By the time I made it back to the village almost four days had passed." Jack gave a soft chuckle and held up his thorn. "My father was so angry he hurled one of these straight for my head!"

Sam's mouth dropped open as Jack continued to grin. "He was a good man, though, my father. My mother died when I was born, after that he did everything he could to keep me close. That's why he'd get angry when I'd wander off, he didn't want to lose me like he did her. If he ever found out that my greatest dream was to leave, I think it would've broken his heart."

"As time went on, he began to lose patience with me and my antics. He got harder on me when I didn't act up to the standards of our 'noble position'. I'd try to sneak away and he'd have guards already waiting to stop me. I was an embarrassment, he'd say, that I was bringing shame to the name of my ancestors. He treated me like a child because in his view that's all I was, and everything I did was a reflection on him. He never thought or cared about what I wanted, all he cared about was honoring tradition."

"One day when I was seventeen, I decided that I'd had enough. I was caught by the guards again, and when I got back my father was in an especially angry mood. He went off about how I needed to get my head out of the clouds, that I had responsibilities to the people, how I was the one who was going to carry on after him and needed to start acting like it. I didn't want to hear a word of it. I was sick of being treated like a child. I told him what I thought of him, of his great proud legacy, and stormed off without looking back."

Sam was leaning forward so much to hear Jack's quiet voice he nearly lost his balance. "That's when you left?"

Jack nodded. "I'd been thinking about it for a while, years at that point, but after the fight that night I was ready to never see this place again. I knew my father would be upset, but this was my dream, and the anger I felt was the spark I needed to make it happen. It was now or never, I remember thinking to myself. I was going to do this, regardless of what he or anyone in the kingdom thought."

"That same night the king was hosting a festival to celebrate the harvest. While everyone was preparing for the party I snuck around the palace gathering supplies for my journey. I took some medicinal pouches and herbs from the healer's chamber, a few rations of food from the kitchens, and a handful of gold to get me by once I'd made it into the world. With everyone distracted I slipped out of the palace and into the forest, for what I thought was the last time."

"I hadn't been gone twenty minutes and the king's guards were on me. I'd almost expected it given the fight with my father, but when they found me they were crazed, furious like I'd never seen before. They tied me up and dragged me back like an animal, and when we got there the entire village was in an uproar. The king was dead, poisoned at the palace just before the festival began."

"Poisoned?" Starlight reflected Sam's surprise.

"That's right," Jack looked bitter. "I'd never seen everyone so upset, people were crying and screaming everywhere... It seemed like they were all angry with me, and when they got me back to the palace I found out why... they thought it was me who did it."

"You? Why did they think it was you?"

"It was easy enough to put together. I already had a long track record as a troublemaker, and everyone knew mine and the king's relationship was tense to say the least. The guards finding me fleeing the scene of the crime with a pocketful of stolen gold and supplies didn't exactly help my case, either." He gave a dark chuckle. "Hell, even I would've thought I did it. At the palace they condemned me without trial, and my execution was set for the next morning."

"But you escaped," Sam was doing his best to process everything he'd just heard. "How did you get away?"

"One of the king's guards was a great friend of my father's. He knew I was innocent, and that night he helped me escape. We made it to the outskirts of the village when we were found by some of the other guards. He held them off and I ran and ran without looking back... I didn't stop moving until I'd made it out of the forest."

"Do you know what happened to your father's friend?"

"Kendu was the most skilled fighter in the kingdom, but he was outnumbered by other skilled fighters who'd just caught him helping a murderer get away. He didn't want to hurt any of them,

104

they were like his brothers, he just wanted to give me time to escape... I'm sure he fought right to his last breath."

"What about your father?" Sam asked. "What did he say when he found out what happened?"

Jack waved an unsure hand then let it plop on his knee. "The last time I ever saw him was our fight."

"I'm sure he knew you were innocent, too."

Jack gave him a halfhearted smile and looked back towards the south. "Not a day goes by where I don't think about that night, those last words I said to him, what a selfish brat I was... I still wonder that if we'd never had that fight, if that one conversation had gone differently, if I ever would've left at all."

"Do you have any idea who really killed the king?" Sam was starving for answers. "Whoever did it must've gotten away with it, right?"

"I have suspicions, but not much else. Ah, who knows and who cares, none of it matters now. In the eyes of the people I'm a traitor to the kingdom. I couldn't go back if I wanted to."

Finally Sam understood. He'd been dying to know the reason behind Jack's departure, but now that he'd heard it he felt guilt at making the man drag up what must have been painful memories.

"I'm sorry."

"What for?"

"Getting framed... Losing everything... I just feel bad I guess."

"Don't. Turned out alright, didn't I? Events could've gone a tad better, of course, but there's nothing anyone can do about it now. In the end, I got what I wanted I suppose."

Sam looked at Jack with a noble face. "When I get there, I'll let everyone know that you were innocent."

Jack shook his head. "For your sake, don't so much as mention my name. If they find out you have anything to do with me you'll be in as much trouble as I would be."

He patted Sam on the shoulder. "You've got spirit like I've never seen, kid. You keep your head up when life's given you every reason not to. That's something you're born with, it's something you can't lose. The world's going to need more kids like you if it's going to stand up to the trouble that's coming."

Sam didn't reply, he just gave a smile and a nod. Jack covered his mouth and gave a silent yawn, then leaned back in his hammock. "Alright, all this storytelling is making me sleepy. Go on and get some rest now."

"Shouldn't you, too?"

"Someone's got to keep watch. Don't worry about me, a few quick catnaps and I'll be right as rain."

Sam took one last look at the stars before making his way down the vines. Their light and Joan's snores led him back to where the others lay. He climbed into his hammock as quiet as he could, looking up at Jack's lookout spot. He thought about what Jack had told him, and what might happen when they finally did reach the village. Sam had no idea what the next day would hold, but then again, he hadn't known what the next day would hold for nearly a month.

# X

Jack woke them just before dawn, looking rested and alert, thorn already in hand. Birdsongs twittered in the fresh forest air as the four of them rose from their hammocks. The primitive weave of vines had given Sam one of the most comfortable nights of sleep he'd had in years. They each grabbed their thorns and climbed down the great tree, then continued south as sunlight began to spread over the vast forest.

Their morning passed with relative ease, the trees growing thicker and closer together as they went deeper into the forest. Jack was scanning every branch and bush, checking behind every boulder and log they passed. After last night Sam knew that it wasn't just the dangers of the forest Jack was worried about. He was sure the man was keeping his grey eyes peeled for hidden warriors as much as he was for razorvines.

"Ugh!"

Joan recoiled as she stepped in a puddle of frothy black mud. They found themselves at the edge of a misty marsh, the sweet scent of the forest strangled by a sour stench of decay. The dead, wilted trees poking from the muck were layered with thick moss and algae. Crooked branches and broken stumps jutted from the black water at sharp angles, looking like the arms of horrid creatures rising from beneath the surface.

Jack took the lead, hopping on broken logs and boulders across the putrid water. Every log and rock in the swamp was slick with slime, making it hard for Sam to keep his footing. Even with his new boots he couldn't stop sliding on every surface he stepped on. He stepped from a rock and walked along a broken log, careful not to fall into the murky black beneath him. The water was too dark to see through, making it impossible to gauge its depth.

The others were getting farther and farther ahead of him as he followed, keeping his eyes on his feet to keep himself standing. Joan looked back at him as she and Thomas walked along a springy branch, the smirk on her face visible even from this distance. "See you at the village!"

Sam watched as she and her brother continued on, her giggling carrying through the swamp. He looked around the black waters surrounding him and saw a thick log floating ten feet away. Gathering focus, he crouched down and leapt, crossing the distance and planting his boots on the log. He flailed his arms for balance as the log bobbed from side to side, the grimy water splashing onto his pants and coat.

Before he lost his balance he jumped again, to a boulder spotted with black mold. He paused for a moment while he looked for his next target, but the only suitable spot was a stump more than twenty feet away. He noticed some low hanging branches ahead of him, their mossy ends tracing the water's surface. Feeling bold, he jumped straight for them, seizing one and swinging toward the distant stump. At the top of his swing he released the branch, dropping down and landing on the rotted wood.

A loud buzzing to his left caught his ear, and he saw a dragonfly the length of his forearm flying straight towards him. He gasped as it whizzed by, its red eyes twinkling as it skimmed the water's surface. The creature buzzed this way and that, mesmerizing him with its array of colors and shimmering transparent wings. It began to fly off when a black, slimy tongue whipped from the water and pulled it under, the buzzing coming to a stop at once.

Sam turned his attention back to the task at hand, not knowing or wanting to know what might be lurking beneath the blackness. He could feel the decomposing wood beneath him staring to crumble and jumped again, clearing another ten foot gap. Joan and Thomas were only a few yards ahead, the sister trying to help the brother along though he didn't seem to need it. Sam closed the distance between them with a few more springs, his movements growing more natural and agile as he closed in on them.

Joan was holding out a hand to her reluctant brother when Sam jumped clear over them, landing on a log a few yards ahead. He jumped again, smiling to himself as he pounced onto another jagged log. Jack wasn't far ahead, moving through the dying trees like he'd practiced the course a hundred times before. Rand was close behind him, but it was obvious the young man was overexerting himself. Sam could hear him panting as he chased behind Jack, his leaps brash and ungraceful in his haste.

Sam continued along, proud of himself for not be trailing behind everyone else for once. Ahead of him Rand continued to fight for the lead, using dangling vines to fling himself farther forward. Sam was closing in on him when he heard Joan scream behind him, followed by a sickening squelch.

"Thomas!"

Sam turned and saw Thomas being dragged across a boulder, a thick, pulsing tendril knotted around his ankle. His sister scrambled towards him with her weapon raised and smoke growing from the fingers of her empty hand. Before she could strike the boy grabbed the slimy appendage and pulled, gripping his sword as the black water splashed. Joan stopped as a spined, toadlike creature the size of a pumpkin was dragged of the water and flew towards her brother, its blank, bulging eyes contracting in the sunlight.

The boy was still on his back as he yanked the creature toward him by its tongue, its short limbs flapping against its round slimy body. When it reached him Thomas slashed with his thorn, spraying himself and the boulder with sticky brown blood. The long tongue slackened as the creature's head bounced onto the boulder, its body splashing and sinking into the murky water.

Jack clapped from a boulder up ahead. "Kid's sharp," he called to Joan. "I'd stick close to him if I were you."

Joan didn't answer. She and her brother were staring at Jack, their faces white with fear. The girl trembled as she took a step back, dropped her weapon and screamed. Jack looked confused as a spitting hiss burst just above his head. He turned to see a gigantic serpent hanging from a tree above him, its yellow eyes fixed on him as it bared its rows of pointed fangs.

He jumped aside as the jaws snapped, the creature's long, patterned body coiling onto the boulder he just leapt from. Jack looked shaky on the algae covered log he landed on, his sword in front of him as he tried to maintain his balance. The creature was more than twenty feet long, its tail tipped with curved spines longer than its fangs. It swung its deadly weapon at Jack, the spikes missing him by mere inches.

Sam wanted to help but saw nowhere safe for him to jump to. Joan was rooted on the spot, holding her brother and cowering on their rock. Rand was closest but stayed right where he was, watching the creature lash at Jack with cold, indifferent eyes. The snake snapped again and again, its triangular head bobbing from side to side as he swung his weapon at the beast. It reared and swung its tail again, forcing Jack to spring upward into the dying branches.

The creature hissed and spit as coiled itself around the trunk, shaking the tree as it started to climb. Jack cursed and walked along a branch near the top as the creature grew level with him. He moved like a monkey on all fours to the end of the branch but the snake slithered out to follow him. Jack grabbed for another branch with his free hand as the tree rocked back and forth, his thorn slipping from his grip and splashing into the water.

The tree began to bend under their weight as the snake reached the end of the branch. Jack leapt over its head to escape when the spined tail swung around and caught him in the shoulder. As he swore in pain the snake wrapped itself around his waist and hoisted him off his feet, its lidless eyes like glowing yellow lamps. The snake spat and snarled as he seizing it by the snout and lower jaw, keeping the fangs off his body as its grip on him tightened.

A heavy chunk of the tree flew as the snake's tail flailed around, splashing in the mud a few yards from Sam. Instinctively Sam jumped for it, skimming it for only a second before jumping to a rock less than the length of the monster from the wobbling tree. The tree shook and swayed as Jack and the snake wrestled, both man and beast refusing to give the other an inch.

Their savage fight soon proved too much for the rotting tree. The brittle trunk snapped in two with a hollow crack that echoed across the swamp. The snake held its grip on Jack as the two fell to the water with a spray of black muck. Sam and the others could only watch as the murky water thrashed beside the downed tree, the snake's tail whipping in and out above the surface.

After a minute the water began to calm, but there was no sign of Jack or the snake. Without a second thought Sam jumped and cleared the distance to the now floating tree. He frantically looked around but the water was far too murky to see anything but darkness. Bubbles started to rise, and Sam jumped back as he saw the scaled crest of the snake's brow break the surface.

His sword was raised at it bobbed in front of him, its eyes blank and forward. He was so afraid that it took him a moment to notice the head was still, and a moment longer to notice it was severed from its body. He stared as it drifted off, and saw a second set of bubbles beginning to appear. Jack gasped as he splashed out of the muck, clutching the tree with one hand, his thorn in the other.

Sam helped him out of the water, his hair and clothes covered in grime. He coughed up some of the black water and wiped his matted hair from his face.

"Damn, that stuff's gross," he said. The swamp soaking his clothes and hair smelled worse than the rankest parts of Farstone's sewers. "I knew one of us was bound to fall in."

The trunk rocked as Joan and Thomas landed beside them, both still pale with fear. Joan stared down at the snake's floating head as if still unsure if it were truly dead or not. The four of them moved fast through the rest of the swamp, and found Rand waiting on a dry patch of forest on the far side.

"So, you made it," Rand said, eyeing Jack's filthy clothes in disgust.

"You sound disappointed," Jack replied. "A little help would've been appreciated."

"I was making sure you were keeping on your toes. For my own safety, you understand."

Jack spat a clump of black on the ground. "I should've left you on that damn boat."

They hurried through the swamp and came to a sandy patch of ground, the only area they'd seen so far without plant life. Sam stepped forward but Jack swung his arm out to stop him.

"Wouldn't do that if I were you."

Rand looked down at the loamy sand soft and prodded it with his blade. "What is it? Quicksand?"

Jack picked up a fist sized rock and lobbed it to the center of the clearing. Sam felt a slight grumble as the sand began to stir and dozens of snakelike creatures plunged out of the sand like it were water. Their heads were featureless except for circular mouths filled with rows of tiny needle-like teeth that jabbed at the spot the rock landed. When they finally dove back under the surface the dirt was left as smooth as it had been moments before.

Jack turned his head at an angle, looking at the sand. "Weird. I expected them to be bigger."

"What are they?" Joan asked.

"Worms," Jack answered, taking careful steps around the clearing.

Joan followed with even more caution. "They sure don't look like any worms I've ever seen."

"Worms, huh?" Sam watched the sand as he followed, intrigued. "You mean like the Great Worm?"

Jack regarded him with an impressed nod. "Well, now, someone knows their history."

Joan looked confused. "I'm sorry, The Great... Worm?"

"That's the everyday term for it," Jack explained. "Its proper name has something like twelve, thirteen syllables, doesn't roll off the tongue quite as easy." He pointed his sword at Sam. "Sounds like you know the story, why don't you tell it?"

"Alright," Sam pulled the book from his coat, turning the pages as he walked. "Remember the story of the Sharpwood Forest?"

"I read the tale on the ship," Rand said, looking at Jack. "The kingdom was under attack by a band of necromancers and their creatures."

"Right," Sam said, pointing back to the book. "The Sharpwood warriors had taken heavy losses, it seemed like there was nothing they could do to stop the skeletons. The king stood on the battlefield with only a few dozen of his soliders remaining. He was ready to lose hope when his warriors brought a prisoner they captured before him. At first the king was ready to kill him, but the prisoner told him that he could help them defeat their enemy."

"The guy you mentioned on the boat, right?" Joan asked Sam, who nodded. She still looked confused. "But what difference could one Strong make against an army of them?"

"He had a power unlike any other Strong," Sam's voice was full of excitement. "Where the necromancers use their power to siphon and destroy life, he could use his to nurture it, to strengthen it. The undead were preparing their final charge when the Strong picked up a dead sapling from the battlefield ground. It was withered and dried, and had worm larvae growing in its roots."

"He fought them off with a moldy tree branch?" Joan smirked. "Quite the plot twist there."

"Not exactly," Sam turned a page. "He used his magic on the larva inside it and a worm burst from it. It grew and grew, until it was taller than the trees, it would've made that snake back there look like an inchworm! The Great Worm wiped out the necromancer's monsters and drove them from the forest forever."

"What happened after that?" Thomas asked, to everyone's surprise.

"After the battle, the Worm burrowed into the ground and a sapling started to grow from the spot. It grew quickly but it only lasted for a minute before it withered and died. The Strong pulled the dry tree from the ground and gave it to the king. Inside was the new larva of the Great Worm. If they ever needed its help again the king could summon it, and a new tree would regrow in its place."

"And all the other guy got out of all that was one of these?" Joan held up her sword. "Boy, did he get taken."

"Does this tree still exist?" Rand asked Jack.

"It's more of a glorified walking stick than anything else," Jack replied. "It was still around when I left, but who knows what's happened since then. Besides, it's just a legend. The village hasn't seen a battle in centuries, as far as I know the Worm's never actually been summoned before. That old log's just a relic the king takes out here and there for special ceremonies and festivals."

They trekked a few more hours before stopping at top of a rocky outcropping, a wide wall of jagged, mossy boulders. "We're getting close," Jack said as they rested at the top. "A few more miles and we'll reach the border of the village."

"Finally," Joan said.

"And then you're turning back?" Sam asked.

"I'll see that you get to the border. Even I'll admit it can be a bit... tricky."

"Tricky?" Rand asked.

"You'll see what I mean. I just hope you can jump farther than what I've seen so far. Hey! Look at this!"

They reached the top of the little cliff, standing in the shade of a wide, wilted looking tree. From its weeping branches hung dozens of plump purple fruits the size of Sam's fist. Jack plucked one and bit into it, purple juice dribbling into his beard.

"I haven't had one of these in years," he said before stuffing the rest of it into his mouth. He plucked two in each hand and tossed one to each of them. They looked reluctant at first, but more than a day without food made each of them take a bite. The fruit was soft and sweet, saturated with sugary purple juice. Sam gobbled his up and reached right away for another. "These are delicious!"

Jack nodded, halfway through his second. "Just don't eat too many, we can't keep stopping for bathroom breaks."

Sam wiped juice from his chin and grabbed another. He wasn't sure when the next time he'd see food would be, so he stuffed a couple in his coat pockets. He reached for more when he noticed a stone at his feet quivering, rocking from side to side like a small creature were pinned beneath it. He turned it over with his boot but saw nothing there but dirt, the rock rolling much farther than the subtle nudge he gave should have pushed it.

It hit another and it too started rolling, then another, and another, prompting others as they moved. The boulders beneath them shifted as more and more rocks rolled after the first. They leapt to the ground as the entire outcropping began to shift, uprooting and swallowing the tree. The boulders reformed into a human-like shape, stone arms and legs protruding from a headless torso.

"What is it?" Sam shouted over the crashing rocks.

Jack was already in a full sprint in the opposite direction. "Not waiting to find out!"

With a thundering of stone against wood the monster chased after them, flinging boulders from the end of its arms at them. One sailed over Sam's head and smashed through the trees in a shower of leaves and splinters. Joan avoided one like a massive spearhead before it skewered her to a tree. Hunks of wood and pebbles rained on them as the boulders tore through the thick, ancient trunks like they were saplings.

The monster flung itself onto its face in an attempt to squash them, missing Sam by only a few feet. The rocks twisted and re-formed themselves into the shape of a gigantic serpent, the boulders now strung one after another. It smashed through the foliage like a battering ram, lobbing rocks at them with flicks of its tail and head. Whenever it passed another boulder it joined the monster, bulking up its size as it pursued them.

Jack leapt as another jagged boulder went right for him. Rand barely managed to duck it before darting away from another, the two rocks colliding in a deafening crash. The five of them moved as fast as they could but the monster was closing in, boulders now launching three and four at a time. Trees crashed down every-where as the rocks ripped through them, forcing them dodge the falling timbers as much as the boulders.

Sam ran alongside the others as more shattered trees fell all around them. He dove behind a broken stump as another boulder crashed past, when he noticed one of the spiny bushes beside him, its sword-like spines quivering. Sam scrambled away just before the spikes exploded in every direction. One pierced a boulder as it flew over him, the thorn sinking deep into the cracked rock.

He felt a pelting rush of wind whiz past him, and a searing pain in his left bicep. Sam glanced down and saw a bloody tear in his sleeve, but couldn't stop to examine it. He started to catch up with the others, doing his best to ignore the pain in his arm. The boulders shifted back into the human shape and began punching and smashing its way towards them, gathering every stone it passed into its lithic form.

Up ahead there was a break in the forest, some wide area devoid of tree or brush. Jack ran straight towards it without looking back, the others close behind. He reached the edge and leapt in mid-stride, the sunlight obscuring him as he landed out of sight. Sam was ready to jump when he saw Rand, Joan and Thomas skidding to a stop at the edge. A chasm more than thirty feet wide separated two sections of trees leading so deep into the earth sunlight didn't reach the bottom.

Jack stood on the other side, waving a frantic arm at them. "Come on!"

With a determined grunt Rand ran and leapt, clearing the distance and landing beside Jack. Grasping each other's hands the siblings leapt, the sister helping the brother along with a forceful tug. Sam stood alone at the crumbling edge, his knees shaking. Behind him the forest was being torn apart, the demonic rock pile drawing closer as Jack flailed his arms and bellowed over the thundering boulders.

"Anytime, now!"

There was no way he could make it; even with his newfound abilities the distance was much too far. Sam thought about which would be worse, getting flattened by a boulder or whatever waited at the bottom of the abyss. He'd had a good run... it was up to the others now to finish what they'd started. He watched them as they shouted and waved him over, looking at each of the four of them in turn. Sam wanted his final thoughts to be of them, the closest thing to friends he'd ever, or will ever know.

Sam could see the others still screaming and pointing behind him, but their voices were strangely muted. It was coming at him, and he knew, he could see it, not with his eyes, but in his mind. He jumped, and a rock twice his height passed right under him. Before it passed he planted his feet on it and dug his fingers in, like he'd done at the Red Ridge. The speeding wind stung his eyes as he hung on for dear life, the boulder carrying him clear across the chasm.

The monster charged over the cliff's edge in a cascade of boulder and branches, no sounds of landing echoing up from the shadows. Jack and the others dove out of the way as Sam flew past them and crashed into the trees behind them. They chased after him down the path cut by the boulder and found it crammed into the base of a tree, its trunk cocked backward from the impact.

Jack grabbed hold of the boulder and heaved it over his head, sending it into the pit with the rest. Sam was lying motionless against the tree trunk, half buried in dirt, splintered wood and leaves. A slight trickle of blood leaked down from under his hat down his cheek. Joan extended a shaking hand toward his lifeless body. "You don't think he's...?"

Sam coughed and sputtered, blinking dirt from his eyes. The rest of them breathed in relief, huddled around him as they helped him up. He felt sticky blood on his cheek and his head was pounding like it was in the Foundry's steel stamper, but by some miracle he made it through the collision in one piece.

"Kid, you are one lucky devil," Jack said. "How in the world did you pull that off?"

Sam looked dazed, rubbing his temple and shaking his head. "Pull what off?"

"If I hadn't seen it, I'd never believe it," Rand clapped him on the back, and Sam staggered to keep his balance. "Well done, Sam!"

Thomas didn't speak but gave an approving grin and nodded. Joan was the only one not smiling. She looked far from impressed, giving Sam a glowering look. "You're lucky to be alive. Next time don't wait until the last second to make your move."

She slugged him in the arm and Sam grasped his bloody sleeve in pain. He'd forgotten about the cut, but Joan had done him the favor of bringing it back to the forefront of his attention. Jack pushed aside the stained fabric and examined the wound. "Not too deep. Wrap it tight and the bleeding will stop, should heal up decent by morning."

Sam's thorn lay on the ground at Jack's feet. He picked it up and handed to Sam, who grabbed it after a few blurry-eyed attempts.

"Well, let's not linger," Rand said. "We must be near the border of the village by now, yes?"

"You'll be there in no time," Jack pointed through the trees behind them. "The gate's about a mile in, head due south and you'll see two big trees, can't miss it."

"So... you're leaving now, then?"

Sam's head was still spinning as he and the others all looked at Jack. Sam had tried his best to make the question sound casual, but he hadn't even managed to convince himself. Jack regarded the four of them with a distant smile, brushing his hair from his eyes.

"You guys don't need me anymore. Hell, I'm not sure you needed me at all. Just keep looking out for one another and you should do alright. I'm still not sure about this scheme of yours... but if anyone could pull something this crazy off, my bet would be on the four of you."

Sam extended his uninjured arm and held his hand out to Jack. "Thank you. For everything."

The man didn't take his hand. Jack's wild eyes were wide with fear, darting back and forth between the branches above Sam's head.

"No-"

Sam heard a muffled grunt from behind him. He whirled around to see Joan and Thomas each being slammed to the ground

119

by two massive, tattooed warriors who appeared from thin air. Before he could react his own legs were swept out from beneath him and he dropped back to the branch strewn ground. A huge hand seized the back of his collar and pulled him to his knees, the blade of a thorn hovering at his throat.

He could hear the others attempting to fight off their captors, but in a few moments the warriors subdued all four of them. Jack knocked one against a tree with a hard right hook, put his knee into the gut of another and took off running towards the cliff. When he reached the edge he leapt, and disappeared into the sunlight once more.

"Wait!"

Sam's words were choked off in the warrior's grip. Another hulk of a man approached him, his voice as menacing as the tattoos lining his brutish face. "You have crossed our sacred border. Outlanders are not welcome in this ancient wood."

"Shall we pursue the one who escaped?" One of the other warriors asked his superior.

"There is no need. The forest will consume him."

"What of these worms?" Sam could feel the hand of the warrior holding him tightening on his collar.

The big warrior looked down at them, his eyes cold and unforgiving between the frightening markings. "Tether them together. The king will decide their fate."

# XI

The ropes dug into Sam's wrists as he was tugged along with the others. Two of the menacing warriors flanked them on either side while the man with the tattooed face pulled their leash at the lead. None of the men spoke, not even to one another, herding the young strangers through the wood in grim silence. The fact that the warriors hadn't killed them outright was a hopeful sign, but the wrong move could change that at a moment's notice.

With every jerking, stumbling step Sam's heart sank deeper with disappointment. In their time together Sam had grown to really respect Jack, despite the others' warnings he'd trusted him with his life. He knew that Jack was afraid to return, but after all they'd been through Sam never thought he would abandon them in such peril. He remembered the seaport, how Jack duped the innkeeper and robbed those three sailors. It looked like Joan had been right all along: Rogues really couldn't be trusted.

"What are we going to do?" He heard her voice whisper behind him.

"Just stay calm," Rand murmured over his shoulder. "If we show no sign of aggression, they'll have no reason to do so themselves. I'll explain who we are and why we've come, once they hear what I have to say I'm sure that they'll be far more welcoming."

Joan stifled a scoff, her voice hushed but frantic. "I just knew something like this would happen, how in blazes did I let myself get talked into this? This was a mistake from the start, didn't I say this was a terrible... Wow."

They stood in the shadow of two gigantic trees, easily the tallest they'd seen yet. Their trunks were covered with carvings, intricate runes and symbols Sam couldn't understand alongside detailed murals depicting battles between warriors and what looked like monsters of the forest. The carvings went so high the uppermost ones blurred together in swirls of vibrant color. A stiff tug on his wrist yanked Sam along as his steps slowed to admire the art.

Beyond them was a grove of ancient looking trees, the lush, vibrant leaves contrasting with the aged bark of their trunks. Sam could make out holes of varying sizes dotting the length of each of them, and they all seemed to have one or more large openings at their roots. As they grew closer Sam realized the holes were beautifully carved windows and balconies, the ones at the base of each became tall, majestic doorways. Hundreds of rope bridges and ladders connected them in a vast network of planks and woven vines.

People were moving about the trees, dressed in simple clothing made from thin fabrics and woven leaves. All the men and women, and even some older kids had the same blade shaped tattoos as Jack on their chests, arms or backs. The villagers watched the warriors passing with their captives, muttering to one another with incredulous looks on their faces. Heads starting poking out of every window, people rushed to balconies and crowded onto bridges to get a glimpse at the strange looking prisoners.

At the center of the village stood a stunning tower carved from a white tree trunk, the roots still deep in the grassy earth. An immaculate courtyard with flowering bushes and stone sculptures surrounded it, split in two by a stone path leading to the palace's tall wooden doors. They were led through the magnificent entryway into a wide, high-ceilinged chamber, bright with sun from the arched windows circling the room. Long gilded tapestries hung from the walls with gaudy carpets lining the polished floors.

The guards brought them before a raised platform, where three more stood on either side of an old man in emerald robes seated on a high backed throne. His face was thin and lined, his beady eyes peering over his crooked, hooked nose. His white hair was pulled back into an intricate topknot braided with jeweled beads and gold rings. One of his talon-like hands rested on the throne's armrest, the other clutched a twisted, withered staff.

The warrior who led them kneeled before the old man and bowed his tattooed head. "The intruders, Your Highness."

"Very good, Marr," the old man replied in a high voice. "Bring them forward."

The warrior yanked them towards the platform. Balancing on his staff the old man got to his feet, his long robe trailing on the floor behind him. He had the appearance of a tall man who'd hunched with age, stooping as he contemplated the four of them.

"Such young faces," he said, leaning on his stick. "I had expected more experienced adventurers when my guards informed me that our sacred borders had been penetrated. I must say, I am impressed indeed that the four of you made it through the Sharpwood Forest with your lives."

Joan and Thomas were watching the dozen or so guards now surrounding them and the old man. Rand stood with his hands behind his back, as collected as if waiting to accept an award. The king paused in front of Sam, each looking into the face of the other. The old man cleared his throat and drew himself up, his joints popping as he stood.

"I am Mornik, ruler of this kingdom. Who are you, young travelers?"

"Well met, good Mornik," Rand stepped forward, his voice clear and authoritative. "I am Rand, prince of the Northern Kingdom. These two are Joan and Thomas from the mountains of the

Everhearth. Sam, ah- yes, Sam here is from a kingdom to the... to the east. We are of the Strong, like you and your people."

"I assumed as much," Mornik's gaze swept across them. "Only a Strong could survive the dangers of our forest, much less cross the depths of the Abyss. Such a perilous journey does beg the question... What could have possessed four young Strong to stray so far from home?"

"Please, good king, we mean no imposition or disrespect coming here," Rand gave a tip of his head, keeping his eyes on the king. "We have travelled far and escaped many dangers to seek an audience with Your Highness, to warn you of a great threat to your kingdom."

The king's brows contracted. "What threat is this?"

Rand kept his voice steady despite the looks from the king's guards. "A necromancer is using an army of undead warriors to wipe out our kind, killing Strong and mortals alike to build his forces as he hunts our kingdoms down."

The old man considered Rand, his jaw twitching. "A necromancer, you say? I thought the knowledge of that black art had been lost centuries ago."

"We had thought so too, Your Highness, until the monsters attacked and destroyed our homelands, and it will not be long before he reaches others. We have made it our duty to warn the remaining kingdoms of this evil. You must ready your warriors and prepare every defense, or your people will meet the same fate as ours."

"I see," the king said, his tone impassive. "Tell me more about this necromancer. Who is he? Where does he come from?"

Rand hesitated for a moment. "Little is known about him," he answered in an uncomfortable voice. "It is unclear where he is from, or where he learned his vile sorcery, but he has vast armies at his command, creatures that do not eat, sleep, or stop until they carry out his orders."

The king's eyes were on Rand with a look of expectancy. "So, this is the reason for your intrusion? To simply relay a warning?"

"Among other things, good king," Rand continued, seizing his opportunity. "This threat is far too great for any one kingdom to face alone. Only by working together will the Strong be able to defeat this evil. We ask that you join us in this, so no more innocent lives are taken, no more of our ancient and noble blood spilled. What say you?"

Rand took a step forward and extended one of his bound hands to the king. Mornik stared down his nose at it, a smug look on his weathered face. "Our blood..." His eyes flicked up to Rand's. "Tell me, Northerner, how many other kingdoms have you managed to recruit to your cause?"

"You would be the first," Rand said, invitation in his words, his hands still in front of him. "Yours is a mighty people, good Mornik, the warriors who captured us prove that. Their skill and speed are unlike any I've seen. The Dark One would be hard-pressed to defeat us with such a formidable ally on our side."

"That much is true," Mornik replied, gesturing at his guards. "Even a handful of my warriors would bolster any force tenfold."

"Beyond any doubt," Rand said with a satisfied grin. "We would spare untold numbers from the tragedies that our people have been forced to endure. So, will you join us?"

Mornik stood in silent contemplation, turning his staff in his fingers. Finally, he looked at Rand with hard, cold eyes. "Your conviction is admirable, boy, but your journey was made in vain. I cannot help you."

Sam blinked. "Why not?"

Mornik glared at Sam, tightening his grip on his staff. "I will not risk the lives of my people for outsiders to whom we owe nothing. We have no interest in involving ourselves in the tribulations of the other kingdoms."

"You don't understand," Sam persisted despite the imploring look from Rand. "They'll find you and you'll all be in real danger. His army could be heading this way right now!"

"I find that hard to believe," Mornik's cavalier tone was infuriating. "Our ancient grove has been hidden for centuries. We are more than well protected here."

"We found you," Sam retorted, abandoning Rand's pompous pretense. Mornik's lip curled into a snarl but Sam was already pressing on. "Please, we need your help. This kingdom needed help once before and someone saved you, someone who didn't owe you anything, didn't they?"

Mornik's eyes widened. "How-"

"Listen to me," Sam nodded at the other three, Rand almost shaking. "The necromancer found their kingdoms, and they were hidden just as well as yours. We've seen what he can do, and if you really care about keeping your people safe you'll listen to what we're saying, Your Highness."

The warrior called Marr stepped to Sam, his knuckles cracking as he gripped the hilt of his blade. "You will address the king with respect, boy."

"Easy, Marr, there is no need for any of that," Mornik placed a hand on the warrior's shoulder and the giant fell back. "...just yet."

"There is more to these children than I had thought," The king looked down his hooked nose at Sam, his grey eyes like dark stormclouds. "Twice I am impressed. Not only did you manage to find your way here you seem quite versed in our histories, as well. Where did you hear that tale, boy? The tale of the Great Worm?"

"I...I read it somewhere."

"Do not lie," The old man's voice was menacing as he gripped his staff with both hands. "I know what you are really after."

"Good king, please forgive my companion's flagrant disrespect," Rand flashed a scathing look at Sam. "He is merely... passionate about our cause. We have come only wishing to help you and your people!"

The king cackled. "Why would outsiders help us? I'll tell you why, because they thought we had something they could take for themselves!" He tapped the base of his staff on the floor and the guards closed ranks around them. "Perhaps some time in my razor-vine pit will coerce the true answer out of you."

As the guards grabbed them the king's grinning face crumpled, his long nostrils dilating as he sniffed the air. "What is that putrid stench?"

They looked up as a shadow moved across the ceiling and dropped to the floor between the entryway and the throne. A figure stood in a beam of sunlight with a thorn in each hand. The man looked around and starting walking towards them, a wild grin shining behind his bushy beard.

"Really like what you've done with place," Jack said as he took in the gaudy rugs and tapestries. "I'm surprised they all don't have your face on them."

The guards let go of Sam and the others, looking back and forth from Jack to the king. Mornik shielded the glare from his eyes with his hand, squinting as Jack grew closer. "What is this? Who in the world are you?"

"Come on, don't recognize me?" "Jack spread his arms like he was offering a hug. "I thought you'd know your own nephew when you saw him!"

The old man's eyes bulged as Jack came to a stop behind Sam and the others. Mornik looked crazed, his face twitching as he stood fixed on Jack. "You...*you!*"

Sam and the others gaped, their heads swiveling from one another to Jack to the king. The old man's knobby fist was balled at his side, his frail form quaking with palpable rage. "I knew it! There was no way outsiders could find their way here on their own! You led them here!"

"They didn't need me to get here," Jack remained casual despite the venom in the old man's eyes. "I was just tagging along, really, enjoying the company... It gets awful lonely out there, all on your own..."

"So," Mornik still looked like he couldn't believe his eyes. "You return with accomplices to try and take the throne, have you?"

"Might have, might not," Jack was still looking around the chamber. "If I were in charge these rugs would be the first thing to go."

"Silence! You have already betrayed this kingdom once, and you betray it yet again by bringing outsiders onto our land! Now you will finally answer for your treasons!"

"We'll get to all that in a minute," Jack put a hand over Sam and Rand's shoulders, his thorns over their hearts. "There's still the matter of my little friends here. They may be annoying and foolish, tedious even at times, but they've done no wrong. You let them go, and then you and I can settle what needs to be settled."

A whistle seared through the chamber and Jack's two blades twirled behind his back in a blinding sweep. An arrow poked from the flat of each blade, their stone tips only just sticking in the dense thorn. He flicked the blades again and fired the arrows at a balcony above the entrance. Surprised cries echoed out as two guards dove into view to avoid them, spilling arrows from the quivers on their backs.

"You're going to have to do better than that," Jack said with a smirk.

"Guards! Seize him!"

Marr advanced on Jack, his own weapon raised. "This is the day I finally end you, traitor."

"Maybe," Jack remained calm but kept his weapons in front of him. "But whatever happens to me the kids walk free. They really did come to warn you, you know. I tried talking them out of it, but they listen to reason almost as well as you do."

128

"Friends of traitors are traitors themselves," Marr spoke without mercy. "They'll suffer the same fate as you, murderer."

"Murderer, eh?" Jack cracked his neck, his eyes growing dark. "You'd know all about that, wouldn't you? Killing four kids should be easy work for you, after you and your pals killed Kendu. Lucky you were all together when you found us, not one of you could've ever taken him on your own."

"No, Marr!" The king roared as the warrior raised his blade to Jack's throat. "I wish to savor his death," Madness held Mornik's eyes. "I have waited ten years for this."

"So have I," Jack said, ignoring the blade beneath his chin. "The kids, Your Highness."

The sets of matching grey eyes were locked with one another. Mornik's cruel face twisted into a sneer of a grin. "Marr, release the children."

The big man blinked in surprise. "Your Highness?"

"Release them and let them leave the kingdom unharmed."

The head guard looked confused, looking back and forth from Sam to Mornik. "Your Highness, they know too much, we cannot allow-"

"You heard me, Marr. Unbind them and get them out of my sight. I have what I want."

The brute looked frustrated, but inclined his head and nodded to a pair of other warriors who untied Sam and the others. Once all four of them had been freed Jack dropped his weapons and the same guards bound his arms with heavy vines. He made no attempt to struggle, never taking his eyes off his uncle.

"You can't do this!" Sam pleaded to the leering king. "He came back to help you!"

"Silence, foolish boy," Mornik spat. "Do not speak of matters you do not understand. I am letting you leave with your lives because you are young and naïve, twisted by the falsehoods this worm has planted in your vulnerable minds. You are fortunate that I am such a merciful and understanding ruler, otherwise you would be sharing his fate as my guard suggested."

"They may be young and naïve, but they were serious about that necromancer business," Jack said as two guards each seized one of his arms. "But hey, I suppose you'll see for yourself soon enough."

The old man laughed, raising his voice and his staff in triumph. "What a glorious event this will be! The betrayer shall finally pay! At last we will have justice for the death of my brother, Tokorro!"

"At least I'll be dead before *they* get here," Jack's eyes were hard as they bore into his uncle's. "I hope you're the first one they turn."

"Still a fool, as always. Did you really believe the tall tales of children, Jakarii?"

"You're going to wish that you did."

Sam and the others stood helpless as the guards took Jack away. As they marched one of them threw a quick fist into Jack's gut, making him drop to his knees. Jack tried to stand when the other guard swung and struck him in the jaw, both laughing as blood sprayed from Jack's lips.

"Jack, don't do this!" Sam pleaded.

Jack looked up at him, blood dripping down his shirt as they dragged him off. "No more hiding for me, kid. I told you the day we left, if I knew I'd sent four helpless, dim-witted kids to their doom I could never live with myself." His smile was red. "Good luck."

They disappeared through an opening at the rear of the room as the remaining warriors ushered the four of them towards the exit. The king resumed his seat and watched them leave, an inhuman twinkle in his storm colored eye. "And be sure they don't try to sneak back in. If they do, we shall have an even larger offering to present."

The guards led them away from the palace, under the continued awestruck gawking of the villagers. When they reached the two carved trees the warriors came to a stop, barring the way with dangerous looks. Without a word the four turned and left, down the narrow path and back toward the open forest. They walked in silence until they reached the end of the path, and the somber quiet was quickly broken by Joan's shrewd ranting.

"Well, that went just great, didn't it? Some real diplomacy skills you've got there, 'Prince of the Northern Kingdom'."

"I would have been able to convince him if someone didn't butt in," Rand flashed an angry look in Sam's direction. "That was a negotiation that required the utmost tact, and you go and insult him the first chance you get!"

"Insult him? He's about to kill Jack!"

"Tough luck for him," Joan stood beside her brother. "I'm a bit more concerned about us at the moment. We came all this way and went through all that for absolutely nothing, and to top things off, we're still stuck in the middle of this hellhole forest!"

"I was marking the trail along the way," Rand said. "At least one of us was thinking ahead."

"Well, the sooner we get out of here, the better," Joan refused to grant him any credit. "Maybe we can find another one of those fruit trees on the way, those things were delicious."

"What are you talking about?" Sam stared at her. "We have to help Jack!"

"He made his choice," Joan looked far past her usual point of aggravation with him. "If he didn't want to die he never should've come back in the first place."

"He just sacrificed himself to save us! We have to do something!"

Rand's lips tightened. "A streak of nobility I'll admit I never expected of him, but as she pointed out he knew what he was getting into by returning, and there's nothing we can do for him now. Let's

131

not make his sacrifice be in vain by putting ourselves in further danger."

"We can't just leave," Sam was not backing down. "We have to go back!"

"Be my guest!" Joan waved at the trail. "Go back there and get your head put on a stake next to his, see if I care! We'd be better off anyway, you and that damn book have been nothing but trouble from day one! If you want to have your stupid little adventure and die a heroes' death go for it, I'm through playing along with your blasted fairytales!"

Branches above creaked as several birds took off in fright at the commotion. Rand took a step toward Sam and put a hand on his shoulder. "We've done our best, we should be proud of all we've accomplished, but this was simply not meant to be. The best thing for us to do now is take care of ourselves."

"I don't believe this," Sam shook his head. "You're giving up, too?"

"This was a longshot from the start, you know that as well as I do. We did all we could, we can take comfort in that, but now it's time to put this behind us. It's time to move forward, Sam."

Sam pulled the book from his coat, his eyes as distant as if he were looking at it from across an ocean. His hands trembled as he stared down at it, turning it over, looking at its spine, the three inches of worn yellow pages cradled between the faded leather covers. It took him only a moment to decide, and once he did he realized he didn't have a second to waste.

He stuffed the book back in his coat and looked around the forest floor, picking up downed branches and swinging them one by one through the air. After discarding a few he settled on a long, springy sapling and trudged off, away from Rand and the siblings in the direction of the village.

"Sam?" Rand called after him. "What are you doing?"

"Moving forward." Sam spoke without looking back. "I'm going to find another way in and help Jack with or without you."

"Are you crazy?" Joan said. "You'll be caught in a second!"

"I have to try. I swore I'd do this and I'm not giving up, even if you all have."

"Come now, this is foolish," Rand said, his derisive voice almost pleading. "You can't do this on your own-"

"Doesn't look like I have much choice, now, does it?" Sam turned back to face them, flinging the words at the older boy in dejected anger. "We all knew this wasn't going to be easy, we knew there'd be danger and risks, and now that we've hit the first road block you're going to just give up?"

"*First* road block?" Joan's eyes burned. "What was the shipwreck, and that horrible snake and those boulders, fun little sideshows along the way? You're trying to act like you're so noble, so brave, but when things actually get tough you hide like a baby and let one of us handle the real danger!"

"I've held my own just as well as any of you, and I don't have half the power you do."

"You're right, you don't. You're just a nobody from a rundown city where no one ever even wanted you in the first place. I don't blame your parents for leaving you at that orphanage, they were probably trying to save themselves from the embarrassment. Go, go ahead and try and save your buddy, he's the only one who seems to give a damn about you." She took a step back. "We sure as hell never did."

She turned and walked away, her face red as her hair. Her brother looked from her to Sam to Rand, then with a hung head slumped off after her. Rand went over to where Sam stood fuming, a calming look on the older boy's face. "Don't listen to her, she's just angry and scared. Just come with us and-"

"Why? I'm just a useless orphan that this whole world would be better off without, right? Don't deny it, I know you think the same thing she does." Sam pushed past him with his shoulder. "Out of my way, I have work to do."

Rand watched him leave. Joan could still be heard yelling as Sam disappeared from view behind a clump of brush. He lingered for a few moments staring at the tangle, then sighed and followed after the girl's voice. His head kept turning back, each time hopeful he'd see something, but the brush stayed still and empty, and after a few more steps he passed a rock and it was out of sight.

# XII

Sam fumbled over root and rock, his eyes swiveling for any sign of the king's guards. He knew that he had to keep quiet, but his frustration was making him clumsy as he blundered his way toward the village. Anger and disappointment were like physical weights on his back but he forced himself to press on. Someone had to if Jack and his people had any hope of survival.

In all the years at the Orphanage, all the days without a single friend, he'd never felt as alone as he did right now. His time with the others had been the first where he felt like he belonged, like he was part of something good. They might have spent most of the time at each other's throats, but Rand, Joan and Thomas, and even Jack had become almost like family- or what he thought a family should have been, having never had any.

Now he found himself alone again, walking blindly through the unknown, the book his only companion once more. He felt lost and confused; how could they have just given up? Their homes were destroyed, their people turned into undead monsters, and when others needed help from the very same fate they turned their backs to save their own skins. If that's how families worked, Sam decided he was better off without one.

There was only one thing left he could cling to in this moment of ultimate despair. He hadn't given up, he knew how important this was. He wasn't doing this for adventure or glory anymore, this was now a mission that kept him going as much as the warm forest air in his chest. Years from now when the three of them thought about what they walked away from, he hoped they could stand the regret.

Holding the book in place he leapt onto a boulder, falling short and sliding down its face. Taking a few deep breaths he tried again, his boots clipping the top but not staying. Growling, he clambered up and lay on his back on its mossy face, his breaths heavy and ragged. He felt more tired than he had in weeks, his limbs weary and sore. The focus he'd had was replaced with a haze, his mind fogged by all that had happened.

There was no doubt the strength he'd felt in the presence of the others was fading fast, and only now was it dawning on him what a dangerous predicament he'd put himself in. Without his power this was the alleys all over again, only here the bullies neared seven feet tall and carried razor sharp thorn-swords. What made him think he could pull this off for even a moment? What if Joan had the real measure of him all along?

No, he thought, that sort of thinking was what made the others give up. They didn't care about anyone but themselves. Jack didn't give up on them and now sat awaiting death because of it. Jack had been there for Sam and the others from the day they'd met, and if Rand, Joan and Thomas weren't going to do anything to save him, he was.

Sam grabbed his stick and sat up, determination pushing through the fog of fatigue. He prepared to slide down the rock's other side when he heard something, a harsh bark that reminded him of Joan's incessant nagging. Crouching beside the boulder, he kept his head down and tried to listen. He heard the noise again and realized it was definitely a voice, rough and commanding.

"Where is this bloody place? I'm sick of this damn forest already!"

136

"Shut it, swine, the map said it'd be right after that big hole."

It didn't sound like a Sharpwood warrior, and it certainly wasn't Rand or either of the siblings. Sam inched forward and peered around the rock, and saw movement in the trees ahead. With his left eye he watched several saplings shift and collapse forward, followed by two large men in heavy black armor. Each of them had gaunt, cruel faces, their spiked gloves clutching broad, rusty axes.

Sam pulled back behind the rock, his heart pounding. He peeked out again and saw the two of them standing in front of the swath they'd made. Sam could hear a distant rumbling from behind them, mingled with the creaking of branches.

One of the men pulled out a spyglass and pointed it south into the wall of foliage. "We're getting close, not more than a click or two away."

"Good thing, too, I'm about ready for some action."

The man pocketed the spyglass and gave his fellow a grin. "Head back and tell Bones to prepare his soliders."

"Why should I go? Send one of them."

The man pointed toward the opening they made in the trees, where two more armored figures were stepping into the light. Their armor was much lighter than the other two, the pale faces seemed to emit a glow beneath their helms. Sam's jaw dropped when he saw that he wasn't looking at faces, but a pair of bare skulls. Skeletal arms hung at their sides, a sword in each of their hands. Their joints glimmered with twinkling blue light, like some mystical adhesive holding the bones in place.

The man with the spyglass stepped to them, staring into their grinning, eyeless skulls. "Ready the troops."

The two skeletons turned and hulked back through the trees. Sam watched the men turn away, one of them keeping his eyes on the monsters as they departed. "Bloody things still freak me

137

out, I'll tell you," his meaty shoulders shuddered. "Fate worse than death, that is."

"Too right it is. That's why Bones is driving us so hard."

"What do you mean?"

"Scuttlebutt among the living soliders says he's awful sore about those kids who escaped a few weeks back. The two redheads and the pale one, remember?"

"I remember, the girl had a mouth on her like a sailor. They were nothing special by my eyes. Bones has killed more powerful Strong than them. What's so important about them?"

"Not sure, but the way I heard it, they were important to *his* boss, and we all know what that means. If *he* finds out they're gone, Bones knows he's going to end up like that," He motioned with his thumb to where the skeletons just stood.

"Wonder what's so special about them," the other replied.

"The Dark One's got his reasons, I'm sure. I'm keeping my eyes open for 'em myself, I'll bet there'd be a hefty bonus in store for the man who finds them."

The two of them set off. Sam needed to get back to the village, now. He moved away from the boulder when he felt a twig snap beneath his foot. He flattened himself back against the rock as the warriors spun around, keeping his breathing as quiet as he could.

"What was that?"

Sam heard their armor creaking, their steps growing closer. "Keep your head on a swivel. Likely they'll have sentries out here."

"Good," The man cracked his knuckles. "I could do with some stretching."

Sam waited in silence for the creaking of armor to pass and fade into the forest. Once it was quiet he sprang to his feet, his chest pounding against the book in his coat. It was up to him, there was no other chance; everything depended on him getting there before those monsters did.

With a tight grip of his stick he turned to run, slamming into a wall of black steel. He fell to the ground and looked up, the blood-thirsty warrior's face leering down at him.

"Well, what have we here?"


Joan stormed her way through the trees, stamping footprints into the ground with each angry step. Rand followed with a defeated gait, moving like he were walking to the gallows. Thomas lagged far behind, dragging his feet across the forest floor. His sister was muttering to herself, as wisps of steam slipped between her fingertips.

"Who does he think he is... thinks he's so great... 'I'm doing this with or without you, I'm not giving up even if you have'... Ha! Damn fool, that's what he is... If it weren't for me he'd be wolf chow, I should've just let them eat his scrawny-"

She punched at the nearest tree, splintering away a chunk of its trunk. She swung again, bashing away another section of wood. She pounded until she smashed clear through the trunk and it toppled in pieces around her. Rand approached her as she panted beside the cracked and twisted trunk, her body shaking.

"This isn't helping."

"Shut it! I'm so sick of listening to you! You and that book worshipping idiot! It's because of the two of you Thomas and I are stuck out here!"

"I'll admit I allowed myself to be carried away by the grandeur of Sa-" The name caught in Rand's throat. "-of the idea, but it's over now. What we need to do now is-"

"I think that was just made that perfectly clear! There's no 'we', there's just me and Thomas, so just stay the hell away from us!"

"Calm yourself, we'll only get through here by working together-"

"Oh, really? Where was that talk a few minutes ago? You don't care about us, you just want us around to help get yourself out of here in one piece!"

"That isn't true," Rand began, but Joan's hard look made him go quiet. The girl was shaking, somewhere between wanting to tear him apart and cry her eyes out. "There is no 'we', and there never was. Let's go, Thomas."

She turned her back on Rand and started towards the chasm. Thomas stood in place, looking at his sister. The girl turned when she didn't hear him follow, the boy's timid, fearful face replaced with one that was hard to read. Without a word he turned and walked away from Joan and Rand, back in the direction of the village.

"Thomas?" Joan looked confused. "Where are you going?"

"Back to help Sam. We all are." The boy's words could have commanded an army.

"What? Thomas, no, he's, he's long gone by now, for all we know he could be-"

"Dead?"

He shouted the word at his sister, whose eyes went wide at the outburst. The boy's freckled face was reddened with anger as he swelled at her. "And it would be our fault! Sam's the one who's kept us all together, he's the real reason any of us are still alive! You called him a coward, but it's you who's been afraid all along!"

Joan stood quaking as she stared at her brother, fire shining in the boy's eyes that his sister had never seen. Rand looked at Thomas as if he'd just noticed his presence for the first time in the entire journey. The boy looked down at is hands and two balls of orange flame appeared in his palms, illuminating the trees as they quickly grew taller than him. He closed his fists and the flames extinguished, looking at his sister.

"No more running away. We swore to do this, and we're keeping our word."

"Thomas!" She called as her brother ran off. "Thomas, get back here! We have to stay together!"

"You're right," Rand said, watching the boy. "You're absolutely right. We have to stay together."

He took off running, taking long strides to catch up with Thomas. Joan stood furious, her fists shaking as the two of them vanished into the trees. "Thomas, get back here! I mean it! There's no way I'm risking my neck again for that sewer-stinking nitwit!"

Sam scrambled away from the warrior, backing against the mossy rock. The man chuckled as he slowly approached. "Well, well, Mort, look what I just found!"

He tried to run but the second brute blocked his way, his weapon resting on his armored shoulder. "What's the hurry?"

Sam stood his ground with his stick held tight, trying to keep his hands steady. The first stepped closer, his axe tight in his grip. "Running off to warn them, are you?"

Sam remained quiet, his eyes darting back and forth between them. The second pointed at him, looking at his comrade. "Thought these people were supposed to be savages, wearin' leaves and such- This one's got regular old clothes!"

"He does, don't he?" The warrior stepped ever closer. "Not from around here, are you, sonny?"

"Sure don't look like it," Sam's eyes flicked to the other, his axe turning on his shoulder. "What are you doing way out here all alone?"

"This raggedy getup looks familiar, don't it?" The other brute tugged at the front of Sam's jacket. "Reminds me of that rathole mortal town we torched a few weeks back. Had loads of fun there, didn't we?"

"Yes sir," The man's evil eyes fixed on Sam. "Now that I'm thinking about it, Bones mentioned a kid he ran into there... Some coincidence, eh?"

Both warriors were right over him now, Sam stooped in their shadows. One of them put their axe up to his throat. "We'll go see Bones and see what he says. Who knows? Maybe he'll recruit you for the...army."

The two each reached for one of Sam's arms when the brush beside them began rustling. They threw him to the ground and readied their weapons, their eyes raking the surrounding trees. One of them swung their blade through brush but hit nothing but leaves and branches. He prepared to swing again when something small in fast crashed into him from behind, driving him against the boulder.

Cold wind sent leaves swirling as a blur of blue dropped from the branches above. One of the warriors swung his axe like a madman as Rand wove around his blows. The young man slid around a sloppy stroke and seized the axe by the handle, yanking it from the man's grip. Grabbing each side of the blade he curled the sharp edges inward and out of harm's way. Rand spun and swung the blunted weapon across the warrior's shocked face.

Thomas was busy fighting off the other, dodging the warrior's relentless axe. A surprise boot sent the boy to the ground, and the weapon went high to deliver the killing blow. Sam charged in to help but Thomas slid under the axe and between the man's legs, pressing his hands against the armor at his back. The warrior screamed and dropped his weapon as the steel beneath the boy's palms glowed red.

Rand continued to fend off his opponent, flecks of blood flying from the man's face as he swung his mailed fists. The man began to give ground as Rand pressed his assault, denting armor wherever his arm or leg hit it. He blocked a heavy punch then delivered one of his own to the man's gut, sending the brute flying back with a metallic clang.

Still gasping in pain, the other warrior released two buckles at his shoulders and the hot panel of steel fell away. Underneath a patch of angry red skin was already beginning to blister. Rand sprang forward towards him, his palms held out at the thug's back. "Let me help you with that!"

A cone of white dust flew at the man, blurring him from view. His scream became a strangled cracking of air, lost in the rush of snowy wind. When Rand lowered his hands and the snow cleared the man was still, his armor and skin a dull, frosty white.

Thomas and Rand ran at the remaining warrior, who was wrestling himself free from a dense clump of vines. He brushed a flower from one out his face as he struggled, the vines coiled around his arms, legs and chest. The two of them had nearly reached him when the warrior was lifted off his feet, screaming as he tried to thrash his way loose. He was consumed in an instant, his cries becoming muffled as the vines covered his face.

His deadened shouts went silent when the vines suddenly pulled tight, the flowers morphed into their razor sharp counterparts. Sam was looking at Rand and Thomas in amazement. Rand returned his stare, his breathing heavy and harsh. "You could have helped at any time, you know!"

Sam's shock quickly turned back to resentment. "What are you doing here?"

"We've decided to finish what we started," Rand replied. "And saving your life, in case you hadn't noticed."

"I thought this was too much for you? Too much for anyone?"

"They were wrong," Thomas approached Sam and held out his hand. "We're not giving up, not now, not ever. We're with you, Sam."

Sam looked at the boy with surprise, then grinned and shook his hand. Thomas looked over his shoulder and called into the trees. "Isn't that right?"

From behind the clump of brush came Joan. Sam was surprised to not see a scowl on her face, but she still looked impatient as she approached him. "Thought about what you said. Thomas and I swore we'd do this, and a Strong is only as good as their word. We're back in."

Thomas gave her a jab with his elbow. Fighting off a wince, she brought her gaze back to Sam. "I'm sorry for what I said. A coward or a fool would never have made it this far, and neither would we if you weren't here. You're as much a Strong as any of us."

Sam watched her for a minute, then smiled and held out his hand. She took it and shook, her eyes holding his. "We're in this 'til the end. I promise."

As they released their grip Sam gave her a questioning look. "How come you didn't help them?"

Joan smiled at her brother. "I promised Thomas I'd let him go this one alone."

Rand had turned away and was now examining the frigid warrior standing a few yards away. "He's only partially frozen. All this humidity seems to be somewhat diminishing my power's effect." He took a sudden step back, his eyes going wide in alarm. "This armor...These are the Bones' men!"

In the distance they heard the thrumming, the steady march of many boots moving through the forest toward them. The four of them glanced at one another with urgent and knowing looks then took off back toward the village, together.

# XIII

Thomas took the lead, the four of them slipping into the village through a field of wheatlike stalks separating the forest from the treehouses. They found the village deserted, every balcony and bridge above them empty. Drums could be heard in the distance, along with savage cries of triumph and anger. Thomas grabbed a tree and started to climb, scaling the branchless trunk with determined ease. They followed him up into the lush canopy, where the shouts and cries shook leaves from their branches.

Hundreds of villagers had assembled, all of them shouting and shaking fists, facing an open circle in the middle of the crowd. A wooden platform stood at the center, occupied by a dozen of Mornik's grim-looking guards. At each end two tribesmen pounded wide round drums, the steady rhythm beating like the crowd's frenzied heart. A pile of twisted, tangled branches sat on the platform, taller than the imposing guards surrounding it.

"It looks like the whole village is here," Sam said, looking down at the massive throng.

Thomas pointed to the edge of the crowd. "Look!"

In the distance the edge of the crowd began to part, allowing a thin figure flanked by more guards to pass through. When man reached the stage the drumming ceased, and the crowd fell silent almost at once. The hunched posture and hooked nose were visible even at this height, and Sam scowled as the familiar shrill voice carried to the treetops.

"Welcome, loyal subjects, welcome to this most glorious occasion! This day is one of great triumph for Sharpwood Kingdom! On this day, we shall have justice!"

The crowd roared its approval. Some of them lobbed rocks at the mass of twisted sticks, leering and shouting curses in its direction. Filled with a burst of courage from some unknown source Sam seized a nearby branch and leapt without knowing or even looking where he was going to land. He swung past another and grabbed hold, surprised at his own daring.

From his new vantage point Sam had a better view of Mornik and the rest of the platform. The branches beside the king were fashioned into a makeshift cage, the limbs woven together as if they'd grown that way from seedlings. He could see a figure standing inside, their face hidden behind a mass of hair and beard. Sam grabbed a branch above his head and he hurried back up to the others, moving even faster than he'd gone down.

"Jack's in there," He pointed at the cage. "They must be about to execute him!"

"They're all about to be executed if we don't do something quick," Joan looked at Rand and Sam. "What should we do?"

Rand opened his mouth to reply but Thomas spoke first. "We have to distract the king and his guards so we can release Jack. Then we can warn the people."

"How do you plan on doing that?" Rand asked.

"You can freeze them, can't you?"

"I can try," Rand looked doubtful, "but with this heat I'd have to be right near them to have any effect. I'll need to get as close as I can."

"Joan and I will create a diversion," Thomas snapped his fingers, sparks flashing in his palm. "You'll have plenty of time to do what you need to do."

"It'll have to work," Sam said. "I'll keep a lookout and see if I can figure out a way to free Jack."

Without another word Thomas dropped branch by branch towards the ground. The others followed, Mornik's nasally voice growing clearer as they drew closer. Just as they reached the ground the crowd roared again, their cries growing more savage with the old man's rallying.

"My subjects, we all remember that fateful day, the day our king was taken from us. This kingdom lost a great leader, and I... I had my brother stolen from me. This traitor escaped justice for ten long years, but now he shall feel the full measure of my wrath!"

Members of the crowd shook spears and thorn-swords as if volunteering to perform the task themselves. Thomas approached a low branch and plucked a few wide leaves, and began wrapping them around his waist.

"What are you doing?" Sam asked.

"We need to blend in, at least for a few minutes. Joan, cover your hair."

In a few moments they looked much less conspicuous, most of their clothing hidden under the leaves. Thomas grabbed a final leaf and folded it around his head, hiding his bright hair. Joan drew her own into a bun and wrapped a leaf over her lead like a shawl. They approached the crowd with quick but casual steps, the people too preoccupied to take any notice.

"Let's split up," Thomas said. "If one of us gets caught the others will still have a chance."

Rand and Sam gave him affirmative nods. Joan looked at her brother with a worrisome look. "You're staying with-"

"Good luck," Thomas said and disappeared into the crowd.

Joan stood staring at the spot her brother had slipped into, then pushed through in the opposite direction. Rand wove into the crowd and then Sam, the villagers too focused on Mornik to pay them any attention. Sam did his best to keep his head down as he tried to reach the platform. Being in the heart of this mass of angered warriors was more frightening than the journey through the forest, and he knew if any of them were spotted, it would not end well.

Mornik jabbed the cage with the end of his staff and the vines retracted, revealing a beaten and ravaged Jack. Even beneath his tangle of hair swollen purple blotches were visible on his face. He was standing tall despite his injuries, but two guards pushed him to his knees. Mornik's gnarled fingers seized a fistful of Jack's hair and held his battered face up to the crowd.

"Look at him, the sniveling worm! He has brought untold shame on my noble bloodline, our sacred forest, and he has insulted us further by daring to return! These were your people, your brothers and sisters, and you betrayed them all!"

The crowd was in an uproar, those closest to the platform spitting in Jack's direction. Mornik threw him back down, his robes sweeping the platform as he paced back and forth, swinging his staff like he were conducting some hellish orchestra.

"I ask you, my subjects, what punishment could fit such a terrible crime? What retribution would be suitable for such a vile coward, who poisoned his own father? My good people, I can think of only one!"

Mornik raised the staff above his head with both hands, and the crowd fell into awed silence. The king nodded to his guards, who hesitated before each taking one of Jack's arms and bringing him forward. Sam edged closer to the platform, nudging through the last few rows of villagers to just under where Jack was kneeling. Every villager had their eyes on Mornik, their faces turning from wondered to nervous. Those closest to the platform stepped back, exchanging fearful glances and murmuring to one another.

Sam slipped under the stage as the villagers retreated, the crowd still circling the platform but at a wider radius. Footsteps shuffled above him as Mornik's guards likewise backed away to the edg-

148

es of the platform. The old man called out again, relish gleaming in his cruel eyes.

"Jakarii the Betrayer, for your crimes against this kingdom I shall unleash upon you our people's mightiest weapon. You will be devoured by our ancient guardian, the Great Worm!"

Shafts of light slipped through cracks in the stage, rippling as Mornik moved back and forth above him. A cluster of vines protruded from the ground a few feet away, growing up and through the planks of the platform. Through a knothole he could see Jack, his face looking worse than ever up close. His bruised eyelids went wide when he noticed the boy beneath him, his battered face incredulous.

Mornik screeched again. "The time has come! Let us prepare the offering!"

"What should I do?" Sam mouthed up at him.

The bloodied lips formed a single word back. *Run!*

Jack disappeared as Mornik dragged him away, their footsteps shuffling over Sam's head. He jumped at a tap on his shoulder and saw Rand crouching behind him, most of his disguise torn and missing.

"Where are Joan and Thomas?" Sam asked.

"They're already in position," Rand said, also trying to peer through the boards above them. "We just need to wait for the right moment, and I'll give them the signal-"

Mornik began shouting indiscriminate words in a bizarre, singing voice. Sam looked at Rand with a terrified face as the king's cries frightened birds from their nests.

"He's summoning the Worm! Do it now!"

"I'm not close enough, it won't work!"

"You have to try! Do it before-"

The king's final screeching words rang out and the two of them heard a heavy thud on the wood above them. Sam threw his arms over his head, expecting the platform to collapse onto them. Moments passed and nothing happened, quiet now filling the tense air. Sam looked up and turned to Rand, who looked as confused as he was.

Mornik shouted more incantations and they heard the thud again, sharper and more forceful this time. The old man grumbled and pounded the bottom of his staff on the platform, but nothing seemed to be happening. Sam peered over the edge and saw him tapping away at the floor like he was crushing insects. The crowd began to whisper as he continued to jab the staff in frustration, his beady eyes fixed on Jack at his feet.

Sam noticed Joan standing at the rear corner of the platform, who nodded then looked past him and gave a thumbs up. On the opposite side Thomas returned it and the two thrust their palms upward. The crowd gasped as two plumes of fire rose up more than twenty feet on either side of the platform. Sam saw Mornik whirl around at the flames, looking shocked and enraged.

The king looked down and saw Sam's head poking out, the wrinkled face twisting with fury. He stormed over to him with his staff held to strike when a frosty blast flew past, the wind knocking Sam off his feet. Rand leapt onto the platform, holding his hands inches from Mornik's chest. Sam Joan and Thomas all climbed onto the stage and helped Jack to his feet.

The ice vanished and the king as still as stone, staff still over his head, his body encased in crystal clear ice.

The villagers had crowded around the platform again, watching them with threatening faces.

"The outsiders!" a man at the front exclaimed. "They're helping the traitor escape!"

"Now they've attacked the king!" A long haired warrior brandished his thorn. "Get them!"

"Please!" Rand called out to the angered crowd. "Listen to me, all of you! We are not here to fight you! Your kingdom is in great danger!"

"What danger?" Another tribesman shouted.

150

"At this very moment an army is marching through the forest to destroy your village. You must get ready to defend yourselves, now!"

An imposing woman at the front stepped forward. "What are you talking about, boy?"

"There is no time to explain, they could be here at any minute! Assemble your warriors, hide your families and prepare for battle!"

A cracking sound came from behind them, followed by a loud crunch. Mornik had broken free of his icy shell, shivering and looking furious. "You meddlesome fools! Guards! Guards, seize them!"

"Are you out of your mind?" Sam shouted at the old man. "Your people are about to be wiped out!"

"Oh, it is you who is about to be wiped out," Guards were already closing in. "You four will join the traitor in the Great Worm's belly."

The guards closed in with swords ready when the drumming returned, though Sam noticed both the drums sitting silent and untouched. This drumming was deeper, darker, an ominous pulse that made Sam feel a chill in the middle of the humid forest.

"What in the...?" Mornik covered his brow with his hand and peered into the distance. The sound grew louder and closer, coming from the trees to the north of the village.

The villagers looked at one another with uneasy faces, taking tighter grips on their weapons. The drumming stopped and everything was still, no eye twitched, no leaf moved, time itself seemed to pause as everyone stared north. A single flaming arrow soared across the blue sky from the treeline, whistling down and nailing the tangle of vines that had imprisoned Jack.

Instantly it burst into flames, its limbs flailing and whipping. They all stepped away as the vines crumbled into ash, and Sam turned back to its source. Men were running towards them through the trees, a pale blue glow visible on the majority of them. Mornik took a wary step back, his hands trembling on his staff.

"What....what is this?"

Jack wiped a dribble of blood from his lips, his swollen grey eyes on the approaching army. "Our worst nightmare."

# XIV

The scene was one of chaos as villagers scrambled around the platform, some calling names of family members, others drawing and preparing weapons. A shrill shrieking was coming from the edge of the trees, where undead warriors were stampeding towards them. Sam looked around for Mornik, who had vanished along with his staff. "Where'd he go?"

"To hide, the cowardly old wart," Jack looked at the four of them through his swollen eyes. "Well, this is it, kids. I hope you're ready for this."

Heavy steps approached Jack from behind. Marr loomed over the five of them, a heavy thorn in his hand. "You-"

Jack stood toe to toe with him. "Assemble your men, Marr, you're under attack here!"

"You filthy traitor," Marr raised his weapon. "I'll dispose of you myself!"

"Don't!" Sam sprang forward as Marr grabbed Jack by the throat. "He's on your side!"

"He abandoned my side long ago," Marr's grip tightened. "He deserves to die!"

"Why do you think he risked his life coming back here? He came back to help you! We all did! Let's fight together!"

The warrior stared at Jack with a calculated hatred, then slowly released his grip. Jack sputtered, massaging his throat as the horde of monsters grew in the distance. Marr drew back his lip and whistled, and men and women began lining up at the front of the platform, warriors each armed with spear, bow, thorn-sword, or some combination of the three.

Marr turned to one of the soliders and nodded Sam's direction, and the man produced swords for each of them. Marr unsheathed another thorn at his back and weighed it against the other in his hands. He settled on the one in his left hand, and to everyone's surprise handed it to Jack. "If remember correctly, you prefer a lighter blade."

Jack took the weapon without a word, a shocked yet grateful expression on his face. Marr was still watching him with malevolent eyes. "I'm not doing this for you. If what the boy says is true then now is the time to prove it. Just know this, if you betray us again or run to save your own hide, I'll take you down myself."

With a bellow like a lion's roar Marr leapt from the platform and charged toward the trees, sword held high over his head. His warriors followed in an earth-shaking charge, leaving the five of them standing alone on the empty platform. They looked at one another as if they were unsure of what to do, or how they got there, or who they even were, but with Jack's wild grin and battle cry they leapt from the stage and charged side by side towards the treeline.

Some of the Sharpwood warriors had already reached Bones' forces and were fending off the fiendish monsters. With the others back at his side Sam felt his strength surging again, fresh and ready to fight as he had ever been. They closed in and joined the fray, one of creatures turning its eyeless gaze on Sam the moment he reached the battle. The skull emitted the piercing shriek and the skeleton charged, swinging a heavy, nail embedded club.

Sam stood his ground and blocked its blow, his thorn slicing clean through the club. The creature swung the remaining half at

Sam, who stepped to the side and severed its weapon hand. It shrieked again before Sam slashed again, cleaving the skull from its shoulders. Another two were already on him, each armed with blood-caked axes. More and more of the monsters poured through the trees, toppling them as they drove their way deeper into the village.

Someone cried out in pain behind him, and he watched as a Sharpwood warrior fell to one of the undead soliders. Another went down a ways off to his left, outnumbered by the creatures three to one. One of the skeletons turned its weapon on Rand, who flipped away from its swing and snatched up the fallen warrior's spear. He spun in a blinding whirlwind, smashing the spear through the skeleton and its two fellows behind it.

Sam jerked his head as an arrow whizzed by, missing him by inches. He ducked and rolled out of the way just as several more cut through where he was just standing. His senses were sharp again, and right then they were telling him to look to his left. Fifty feet away a skeleton aimed a heavy crossbow at him, a fresh bolt already drawn. It came straight for him when a sword flew across its path, slicing the arrow in two before shattering the ribs of another skeleton.

Jack ran at the soulless archer and kicked it to the ground, pulling his sword from the other as he passed. Fighting seemed to come as naturally to Jack as flight did to a bird. He was constantly picking up and discarding dropped weapons, leaving a thorn in a breastplate to throw a stolen spear, then hacking through a pair of skeletal legs with an axe. He took down two monsters for every one Marr's warriors did, and their subtle sideways glances at him as he broke through skull and bone showed that they were taking notice of it.

More of the black armor funneled into the area, the air filled with smoke and wailing shrieks. Sam dodged a swing from another battle axe, causing the creature to cleave one of its own comrades at

155

the shoulder. Its iron covered legs stumbled around like a drunken man before Sam grabbed them at the waist, tossing the bony timbers into another. He grinned at the explosion of bone and steel, just missing another axe blow in his quick lapse in concentration.

The monsters pressed their attack as more and more poured of them out of the trees by the minute. The Strong were taking down scores of them, but for every one they destroyed it seemed two more came charging out of the forest. It wasn't long before the village was overrun with skeletons, the kingdom's warriors forced to regroup as the creatures gained more ground through their sheer numbers.

Arrows rained down from the treetops, the feathered bolts sinking into armor and empty eye sockets. Skilled though the Sharpwood archers were, arrows did little against fleshless opponents, merely disorienting them while a warrior on the ground dealt the finishing blow. Skeletons were scaling the giant trunks and attacking the archers, knocking them from their perches and taking their bows. Now arrows were being trained on the warriors on the ground, who now had to defend themselves from above as well.

Skeletons were igniting torches in the treetops, lighting their arrows ablaze and firing them into the fight. Some of them aimed theirs into windows and balconies, and soon several of the giant treehouses had caught fire. The flames began spreading to the surrounding trees, heavy smoke billowing through the grove. Hiding villagers scrambled onto bridges away from the blaze, screaming for their lives as the flames flushed them out.

Sam saw Jack heave a spear into the chest of a skeleton, then swing the sword in his other hand to cleave off its head. Sam dashed over to him, weaving around swishing swords and arrows coming from every direction. "There are too many of them!"

"I've noticed!" Jack batted a helmeted skull off one skeleton, sending it smashing through the rib cage of another. "We need to find Mornik!"

"Why?" Sam dodged a skeleton's sword then cut through its legs with his own. "What do you need him for?"

"His staff, I need his staff to summon the Worm!"

"But it didn't work!" Sam dodged another arrow.

"I have to try it's the only chance we've got! I know where he'd be, let's get to-"

The wind whistled as more arrows whizzed past, one of them sinking into Jack's shoulder. Despite the injury he managed to block two more with his thorn before diving behind a tree. Red spread across his shirt as he yanked the arrow out, staunching the wound with his free hand.

"Are you alright?" Sam watched blood leak between Jack's fingers.

"I'll be fine," Jack grimaced as he kept pressure on the wound. "The palace, let's go."

Sam followed Jack through the chaos as the warriors continued to fight off the sea of bones and black armor. The battle hadn't reached the palace grounds yet, the stunning white tower and surrounding courtyard remaining pristine and abandoned. Jack flung the doors of the palace open and the two of them dashed down the hall to the empty throne room. Dark clouds had replaced the sunlight in the windows, the sounds of the battle coming through them.

"Where do you think he is?" Sam asked, glancing around.

"He's got to be around here somewhere," Jack winced, keeping his hand at his chest as he looked for any sign of his uncle. "He couldn't have gotten far..."

The shouts and screeches of both sides could be heard in the distance, along with the clanging of weapons against armor. Sam started to search when he heard a gasp and saw Jack stagger into the wall. Sam thought it was the pain from the arrow, but Jack's hands were at his temple, breathing heavy and shaking.

"What is it?"

"I... feel it again," Jack whispered. "The cold...inside..."

157

As he grunted footsteps came from the hallway across from them. Sam threw Jack's arm around his shoulder and led him behind a large ornate vase. The slow, heavy steps grew louder, echoing off the high tapestried walls. Jack leaned his back against the wall and clutched his chest, his breath coming out in steam like it were winter. Sam noticed his own breath steaming as he felt the temperature drop around him.

He peered around the vase and saw a hooded figure walk into the room, moving slowly towards the center of the chamber. The figure's boots tracked mud onto the polished floor as they took in the decorations, a rasping chuckle coming from behind the hood. Sam knew that sound, he'd heard that horrible laugh once before: in the alley between Stone & Stone and Martin's Alehouse.

"It's Bones!" Sam whispered to Jack.

Jack put his finger to his lips as he tried to steady his breathing. Sam turned back and saw Bones had removed his hood, and was now standing beside Mornik's throne. He looked even paler then Sam remembered, the grey skin of his sunken face barely clinging to the skull beneath. Bones reached out a thin hand and stroked the armrest of the throne, his long fingernails scratching the wood.

Sam saw him spin suddenly away from the throne, his skull-like face turning in their direction. He smiled and strode towards them, his boots echoing again through the silent chamber. Sam ducked behind the vase and crouched as low as he could, his sword at the ready for the moment Bones reached them. Sam was puzzled when the footsteps marched right by them and continued across the room. He stuck his head around the vase a fraction of an inch to see what could have caught the cadaverous man's attention.

Bones stood a few yards away from them, in front of one of the gaudy tapestries. It was quivering slightly, and Sam could see a lumpy mass protruding behind the cloth. A grey hand reached out and tore the fabric aside, revealing a crouched and cringing Mornik.

The king clutched his staff in his arms like a frightened child cling-ing to a parent's leg.

Bones laughed as he looked down at the cowering king, the tapestry dropping to the floor beside them. He lifted his hand and Mornik rose to his feet with a yelp, lifted by some unseen force. The old man gripped his staff in his trembling hands as Bones looked him over, his yellow eyes gleaming.

"Ah, the king, I presume?"

"Please!" Mornik's voice was high and cracked. "Do not harm me! Have mercy, I beg you!"

"That shall depend solely upon you." Bones turned away and raised his hand again. "Come, my friend, you and I have much to discuss."

Mornik gasped as he was pulled forward, the toes of his pointed shoes dragging on the polished floor. Bones led him back to the throne and turned to face the king. He lowered his hand and Mornik landed on his feet, his grey eyes wide with fear.

"Who are you?" The king asked. "What do you want?"

"I am glad you asked. My name is Bones, and I am here on behalf of my master to accept the unconditional surrender of your kingdom." His hand stroked the back of the throne. "I trust that you will make the rational decision here."

"I-"

The hand behind the throne made a fist and Mornik was lifted up again, gasping for air as his staff clattered to the floor. Bones smiled as he watched the old man struggle, his face looking more skull-like than ever. "It is not a difficult question, a simple yes or no will do."

"Y-yes," Mornik choked, his legs kicking as he hung in mid-air. "Please-"

"Good," Bones dropped his hand and Mornik fell in a heap of green robes. "I thought you would see things my way, with the proper persuasion."

Bones turned and examined the throne again as Mornik got to his feet. "My master will be pleased that we reached an understanding so quickly. I must say, you are the first to submit to the Dark One's will with such minimal protest. Wise indeed, to not cross a necromancer, good king."

"N-Necromancer?" Mornik whispered.

"Your new master, as you will henceforth refer to him. Unless, of course, you have some issue with that?"

"No," Mornik held out his hands and bowed his head before he was lifted up again. "I-I am eager to serve!"

"A wise choice," Bones settled into the throne. "It would be a shame if you were to perish over some foolish sense of pride and honor, as those defiant kingdoms before you have." He went quiet for a moment, allowing the din of the fight outside to fill the room once more. "Your warriors fight valiantly. They will make a fine addition to the Dark One's army."

"Yes, yes," Mornik gave another tilt of his head, looking somewhat relieved. "T-they are his to command!"

"I would hope so," Bones allowed the sounds of battle spiral in the air once more. Sam could hear cries of pain, and saw flashes of orange light glowing in the windows behind him. "These men and women fight for their homes, their families... their king." Bones' grin widened. "Warriors of such integrity and resolve are not so easily made to surrender. How can you be sure they will serve my master?"

"They will surrender, I assure you," Mornik said. "They believe and obey my every word!"

"I hope you are right for their sake, and your own. My master does prefer to keep new recruits as they are, but he is more than willing to us the... alternative where necessary."

Mornik jumped as a shriek from one of the skeletons rang through the chamber. The battle had reached the grounds of the palace, the sounds of the assault coming from the courtyard outside.

The king did not look the least bit concerned for his people, nodding to the grinning man before him. "They will surrender or die!"

"In either case, they will still serve my master. As will you, should you ever have a change of heart."

Jack moved away from the wall and peered around the other side of the vase. Mornik's staff was lying on the floor behind the old man. Sam could see the anger on Jack's face as he looked from the staff to his uncle to Bones. Mornik seemed less afraid now, ignoring the staff as he listened at the man in his throne.

"It is time for you to give your last order as ruler of this kingdom," Bones said as the sounds of combat grew closer outside. "You will address your soliders, and order their surrender."

Mornik nodded. "And, what will become of me?"

"That will be up to my master. He often spares those who have shown loyalty to him, but I myself can make no guarantees."

"I will be a great asset to him," Mornik replied. "I may be an old man, but I am cunning and capable as any."

Bones sneered. "I could see that, by the way you were cowering behind that curtain while your warriors fought and died for you."

Mornik gave the slightest grin. "You underestimate me, my friend. My skills lie outside the realms of physical prowess and brute strength. It was through cleverness and guile that I came to rule this kingdom, and having the courage and will to seize what was mine."

"Is that so?" Bones looked as skeptical as he did amused. "And just how did you manage that?"

"Before I came to power, my elder brother was ruler of this kingdom. He had ruled well for nearly eighty years, but age was getting the better of him, and his health began to degrade. It was his wish for his son to take the throne after him, but the boy was an insolent fool, unfit to rule a colony of insects let alone a kingdom of the Strong. The kingdom needed a powerful, wise leader if it was to strengthen and flourish."

161

"And that would be you, I take it?" Bones leaned back in the throne. "Please, do go on."

"On the eve of our great harvest, my brother had a heated argument with his son and came to me seeking my counsel. He was gravely disappointed in the boy, but still believed that in time he could learn his place as king. His caring for his only child had clouded his greater judgement. I could not allow control to fall to the whim of a lazy, disobedient brat. Before we left for the festival I offered my brother a goblet of wine, spiked with a mild but effective poison."

"You poisoned your own brother?" Bones raised his eyebrows.

"I did what needed to be done, for the greater good of this kingdom. The poison I used was carefully brewed, and brought him a peaceful, painless death. I did not wish him to suffer, but his time as ruler had come to an end."

"And no one suspected you?" Bones watched the king from his own throne. "Not even his son?"

Mornik looked pleased with himself. "I had overheard the argument between the two of them, which had taken place in this very chamber. I intercepted the foolish boy as he stormed out of the palace. He was angry and willful, and wanted to flee his responsibilities like the cowardly child I knew him to be. I realized that this was my opportunity to assure the kingdom would rest in the hands of a worthy ruler."

"I provided the boy with a sympathetic ear and some words of encouragement, and helped him flee the grounds in secret. When his father was gone I alerted the palace guards to what I'd seen, that I'd heard the boy shouting in rage at the king less than an hour before, and witnessed him sneaking out of the palace soon after. It was well known that the brat hated his father, and would do anything to be out from under his thumb. As far the guards were concerned it was obvious the boy was the murderer."

162

"Interesting," Bones approved. "It would seem you understand what is necessary to achieve a higher aim."

"On the path to power, all are disposal." Mornik's beady eyes twinkled. "I don't think it ever even occurred to the boy that it was I who'd done it. Had he not been such a fool, he might have known better."

Jack was shaking beside Sam, his face contorted with rage. His eyes were fixed on his uncle with a seething hatred, his bloody teeth gritted like a rabid animal. Bones considered the king's words as the battle raged outside, the courtyard filled with shouting and screeching. "I will speak to the Dark One on this matter. I think he will consider you to be a more than adequate lieutenant. Great power and reward await those who serve at his side."

Mornik nodded again, a satisfied grin on his weathered face. "It is clear to me he is the new great power in this world, and I would take my chance to share in it."

Mornik extended his hand, which Bones grasped in his own skeletal claw. Mornik took to one knee and bowed his head low. "I hereby swear my undying loyalty, as well as that of my people. Anyone among them who challenges this shall meet whatever fate our master deems fit."

"He will be pleased indeed." Bones' eyes were glowing with delight as the king got back to his feet. He rose from the throne and placed a hand on Mornik's shoulder. "Now, let us bring this pointless fighting to a close."

Jack was taking short, heavy breaths, his sword shaking in his grip. Blood from his chest had smeared onto the vase and was dripping onto the floor. He swayed back against the wall once more, clutching his chest in anguish. He looked at Sam, who could see the anger and pain in the wild grey eyes. Jack steadied his grip on his weapon, and without a word to Sam sprang out and charged at the two men.

Mornik whirled around as his nephew rushed at them, roaring at the top of his lungs with his blade held high. Bones chuckled and raised a withered hand in Jack's direction. Jack froze in place, a glittering blue aura surrounding him. He was lifted off his feet and with a flick of Bones' wrist Jack was flung backwards through the air. Jack cried out and landed on his back near the fallen tapestry.

"What do we have here?" Bones said.

"A traitor," Mornik pointed a crooked finger at Jack like a tattling schoolchild. "He has come here to stop you, My Lord!"

"Has he now?" Bones grinned as Jack got to his feet, his sword held in front of him. He made a swatting motion and the sword flew from Jack's hand. Jack was lifted again as Bones clenched his fist and walked towards him, Mornik sneering at his heels. "He will make a prime example of what will happen to those who dare oppose the Dark One."

"Yes," Mornik laughed. "He and his band of meddling children have been conspiring against you-"

"Children?" Bones' face snapped toward Mornik. "What children?"

"There were four in all, My Lord, a young man with long hair, a slight, smart-mouthed boy and two red-headed siblings-"

Bones spun away from Mornik and crossed to Jack, pulling him in with a swing of his fist. Sam saw Jack skidding across the floor surrounded by the blue light, writhing and groaning before stopping at Bones' boots.

Bones squeezed his fist and Jack screamed in agony. "Where are they?"

The two stared at one another, yellow and grey boring into one another. Jack stopped struggling, as his grimace changed to a grin. "Do your worst."

Bones snarled and clenched his fists. Jack began to convulse as the blue light surrounding him flashed and filled the room. Sam was too far away, if he tried to run at Bones Jack would be dead and worse long before he reached him. As he stood pressed hopelessly against the vase he felt a lump in his coat, only it wasn't the book. He plunged his hand into his pocket and pulled out stained purple fingers, one of the plump, sweet fruits from the forest sitting in his palm.

Closing one eye and lining up his best shot, Sam lobbed it with all his might across the throne room. The fruit sailed through the air and found its mark, splattering against Bones' pale temple. He staggered sideways and Jack dropped to the ground, and snatched up Mornik's staff before his uncle could react. He sped from the room, moving in the blink of an eye past Sam through the exit. Sam raced after him and Bones and Mornik followed, both men shouting curses after them.

The battle was raging just outside the palace doors, warriors and skeletons alike tearing each other apart across the courtyard. Three figures raced towards Sam, almost unrecognizable covered in the grime of battle. Rand had a deep gash in his forearm and a bloody stain on his right leg. One of Thomas' eyes was swollen and his lip was bleeding, and Joan had an arrow shaft sticking out of her back near her shoulder, her hair and face caked in mud.

Jack gripped the staff and began muttering under his breath. Sam and the others surrounded him, keeping the skeletons off him as the incantations streamed from his lips. Bones and Mornik burst through the palace entrance, leering like demons at the five of them. Jack held the staff up in front of him, whispered a few final words, and then slammed it down into the dirt.

The fighting paused as the ground began to quake, the surrounding trees shaking from root to branch. Jack released the staff and backed away from it, the stick remaining on its end and quivering in place. A squelching, cracking sound was coming from the twisted bulb at its end, which twitched and broke open in a spray of splinters. A thick, pulsing larva landed on the ground, its fluorescent green skin spotted with brilliant red and yellow spots.

It burrowed into the dirt and the ground shook even more, a mound growing from the spot where the worm vanished. The pile of dirt grew to twenty feet high in a matter of seconds, spreading wider and taller with each moment. The four children, Jack, Bones, and Mornik all backed away as the undead creatures blindly charged up it. At close to forty feet in height the mound stopped growing and the ground went still, and dirt exploded into the air like a volcano.

Sam brushed grit from his face, deafened by the rumbling in front of him. A worm the size of one of the giant trees came sliding out of the ground, its brightly colored body over a hundred feet long. It coiled and loomed down like a cobra as long black spikes began to sprout from its back and sides. Its head was featureless like the other worms they'd seen, its massive, needle filled mouth letting out an ear shattering roar.

With one glance from the others Sam ran as fast as he could as the worm turned on the horde of undead. It roared and whipped its spined tail, swatting dozens of the creatures away with a single swipe. Every skeleton turned its attention to the worm, their shrieks mingling with the titan's bellows. Some of the monsters latched onto the worm and began climbing its slimy body, only to be impaled by spines stabbing from beneath the worm's skin.

Pandemonium reigned throughout the courtyard, the sea of skeletons charging the worm, the remaining Sharpwood warriors doing their best to avoid being trampled by either. The gargantuan beast pushed back the undead, whose attacks were having as little effect as rain on a mountain. Warriors flung spears and fired arrows at the monsters from the sidelines, keeping a wide distance from the range of the worm's teeth and tail.

More and more of the skeletons climbed up the worm's body, hacking and stabbing into its fluorescent skin. It bucked and thrashed to shake them loose, but more and more climbed up to take their places. The worm began firing its barbs into the horde on the ground, causing explosions of dirt like cannon blasts. Skeletons continued to hack and slash at it, a dark blue fluid leaking from the stabs and cuts to its body.

The worm swayed, undead warriors losing their grips and falling onto their fellows. It let out a mournful call, looking unsteady as its head started to rock back and forth. The guardian looked as though it was about to topple with it let out another roar, and shook the skeletons off its body. It closed its mouth and looked down at the ground, a humming sound coming from the worm as its spines began to glow.

A beam of energy bright as sunlight fired from the worm's mouth, incinerating the skeletons the instant it passed over them. It moved its head back and forth, purging the undead creatures in its light. Sam heard curses and saw Bones staring at the worm with a look of incredulous rage. For a moment he looked at Sam as if he were going to charge at him, but with a rush of wind the man's cloak dropped to the ground, and an ugly white bat took off into the sky, over the trees and out of sight.

The skeletons continued to attack down to the last few of them, the bone burned away by the dazzling beam. When the last one disappeared the worm closed its mouth, and the beam vanished in an instant. The ground was scorched and smoking, without a single skeleton in sight. The worm threw back its head and roared once more, and the villagers on the ground and in the trees all did the same.

Everyone was cheering and shouting, families were running to rejoin their battered soliders. Sam and the others leapt up and down in a circle, whooping and clapping each other on the shoulders. Jack limped over, coughing a little as he did so, and joined them. Their celebration was stifled when Marr approached them, his hard face unreadable. The crowd fell silent at a high pitched voice shouting over them, and a disheveled Mornik leapt on top of a rock and addressed the crowd.

"My loyal subjects, thanks to me, our enemy has been defeated! Using spells passed down by my ancestors, I summoned the Great Worm-"

"You didn't summon it," Sam was surprised to hear Marr speaking to the king in such a threatening tone. His ember-like eyes were fixed on the king as he pointed his sword at Jack. "He did."

"Don't be ridiculous," Mornik's eyes flashed. "I summoned it moments ago-"

"I saw it with my own eyes," Marr took a step closer, his sword gripped tight in his hand. "He summoned it, while you were surrendering us all to that grey-faced demon!"

"Who do you think you are speaking to?" Mornik's voice was shrill. "I am your king!"

"You are no king," Marr was looking at Mornik like he had at Jack just hours previously. "I followed Jakarii and the boy when I saw them heading to the palace. I heard you selling us all to that monster, I heard everything! You poisoned Tokorro, and framed his only son for it! It was you, all this time it was you!"

"You are a madman!" Mornik exclaimed. "A liar and a madman! Guards, seize him!"

"You can't trick your way out of this one! You killed your own brother, and would have killed your nephew too, all for your own gain! You forced me to kill a great friend, and I thought him a traitor for years! You are unfit to breathe the air of this forest!"

Marr was about to swing when a shadow passed over him, casting both he and the king beneath it. The worm swung its tail over them and jabbed a spine through Mornik's gut. The old man's eyes bulged as he was lifted off his feet and brought over the worm's head. It opened its gaping mouth and dropped him in, his feeble cry stifled when it closed around him. The worm let out a rumbling croon, and fired another beam of blinding light into the sky.

The clouds began pouring rain, dowsing the village and extinguishing the burning trees. With a final guttural call the creature

168

plunged its head downward, diving into the muddy ground it came from like water. The dirt sealed after it disappeared, leaving a wide, flat plot of loam. A leafy sprout poked out of its center, growing until it formed into a lush six-foot tree with wide red and yellow leaves.

The leaves wilted as quickly as they had grown and the branches crumbled away, leaving behind a thin withered trunk. It swayed in the rainy wind before toppling with a soft thud, a gnarled knot on its end. Marr stepped forward and stabbed his sword into the mud, then stooped and picked up the dead tree. The people watched as he walked back over to them, then bowing his head, he held it out to Jack.

"Only the true king can summon the Great Worm," the warrior said, then took a knee at Jack's feet. One by one the members of the crowd dropped to one knee facing Jack, who looked like he couldn't believe his eyes. He looked down at the staff in his shaking hands, tears trailing along raindrops down his face.

Sam and the others looked at him with beaming faces, and with a shout of joy Jack held the staff high over his head. All at once the soaked crowd leapt to their feet, cheering for their new king. The four of them rushed forward and threw their arms around his shoulders. He winced in pain and shrugged them off, still laughing and beaming down at them. The four of them bowed their heads and he did the same to them, joyous tears trickling into his beard.

"So what now, Your Highness?" A smile shined through the filth on Joan's face.

"I'll tell you what now," Jack gave them an exhausted grin and let himself fall onto his back. "A brandy and a bed."

# EPILOGUE

Icy wind from the north whipped the tower, the light of the half-moon pouring into the topmost chamber. The tiny space was cold and empty, the wide, glassless windows open to the night air. Stars twinkled against the dark blue backdrop, the night sky free of clouds. A figure stood gazing out one of the windows, shrouded under a grey cloak.

Movement caught the stargazer's eye as one of the distant stars began to move, growing larger as if hurtling towards the tower. As it grew closer it was clear that it was no star, but some flying creature. Red eyes gleamed as the white bat closed in, swooping down and flying through a window. The wings and legs grew and the face contorted and stretched as the beast transformed into a pale, desiccated man, who strode toward the cloaked figure with purposeful steps and dropped to one knee.

"Master," the man said, his lank white hair hanging past his face.

"You return early," A voice spoke from beneath the grey cowl, back still turned to the man on his knees. "You have taken the Sharpwood Forest sooner than I would have expected."

Bones stayed on his knee, keeping his eyes low. "My Lord, I regret to inform you that I have yet to -"

A chill rushed through the chamber. "Then why are you here?"

Bones swallowed before answering. "I admit I underestimated their skill, they had defenses I was unable to anticipate. I have come seeking additional forces-"

"Additional forces?" The man beside the window turned and looked at the man on the floor. The hood kept the face hidden in the shadow beneath it. "Five thousand soliders were not enough to dispatch a few scores of woodland savages?"

Bones shivered and spoke with his eyes on the stone floor. "My Lord, they summoned some kind of monster, this-this horrible creature that wiped out my army with its-"

"Spare me your excuses," The cloaked man stood an inch from Bones, wind whipping through the freezing room. "Half that number should have been able to ambush them without fail."

"They were prepared for our attack, they were warned of our approach-"

"How is that possible? Warned by whom?"

Bones had been dreading this moment for weeks. "It was the children, my Lord, the boy from the North and the two from-"

Bones choked on his words, rising to his feet before being lifted off them. The hooded man's sleeves were joined in front of him, watching Bones struggle from beneath the hood.

"You've let them escape?"

Bones' limbs began to twist as he struggled for breath. "My Lord- please-"

"I am disappointed indeed... My most trusted general, thwarted by primitives and children..."

"Forgive me, my Lord...Send me back, I will destroy them..."

The man turned away and Bones dropped to the floor. Moonlight covered the cloaked man as he gazed out the window, the thin grey fabric trailing in the wind.

Bones stepped towards him, looking fierce and determined. "Give me two legions of undead and I will bring the forest to its knees. As for the children, I shall bring to you their heads."

"No," the cloaked man said. "I want them whole and unharmed." He stood listening to the wind, then turned and looked out another window, his hands still joined in front of him. "They are rallying the remaining Strong... This changes things," the man continued after another pause, more to himself than his inferior. "Our time frame has accelerated..."

"I can return to the forest in days, I need only the soliders," Bones snapped to attention. "Three legions should be enough to overwhelm and obliterate them once and for all!"

"The forest does not concern me at the moment. These children are a threat to my plan. They must be stopped."

"Understood, Master. I will not fail you again."

"I am sure of that," The cloaked man said. "I will have another attend to them for now. I do have one small task for you at the moment, though, my old friend. I trust you can handle it."

"Of course, My Lord, whatever you-"

The lieutenant was yanked forward as an ashen grey hand seized him by the throat. The cloaked man brought the grey face to his hood and breathed deep, raging gusts whipping through the tiny room. Bones went limp as his body shrank and withered into a desiccated husk, the skull rolling back on its bony neck.

He heaved the corpse out the window, watching it plummet into the darkness. His gaze turned south, watching three red stars twinkling just above the horizon.

"Where will you go next?" The necromancer whispered to the wind. "We shall see soon enough... wherever you go, we will be waiting."

Enjoy an exciting excerpt from
Part Two on the following page!

Sam took a drink of water, sweat crowding in fat beads on his forehead. He forced himself to stop before finishing it, not sure when the next time he would see more would be. His eyes stung as he squinted down at the map in his book. The sunlight made following the instructions on the page difficult, as did the gritty breeze in his face. The dunes were featureless around him, no sign of any settlement or structure, only miles of empty sands.

"How much further?" Joan panted behind him.

"We should be getting close," Sam pulled his cap low to shield his eyes as he scanned the endless sands.

"You said that two hours ago," Joan muttered, dabbing sweat from her face. "Where is this place already?"

"We just have to keep going. According to the book, 'the tower lies in the path of the setting sun.'"

"We hope," Joan said. "That book is old as dirt, we don't even know for sure if these people still exist. For all we know this tower could've fallen over, or been buried out here centuries ago."

"No," Sam said. "There's something here, I can feel it."

"All I feel is that miserable sun," Joan said.

Sam knew she was skeptical about the spirits of the desert, but he could feel a power in the sands, a burning that had nothing to do with the heat. Pushing his fatigue aside, he hiked his pack up on

1

his back and pressed on toward the west. "Let's keep moving. We're not going to find it standing here sweating and complaining."

Any sign of the forest had long vanished behind them. The two places were so different they might have been on different worlds. Where the forest had been teeming with life the desert was empty and desolate, without a single shrub on the dry, infertile ground. There were no hidden dangers of razorvines or snakes lurking behind the next boulder or bush, an advantage Sam was thankful for. Not only that, if they did run into any of the Dark One's warriors out here they would see them coming a mile away.

Still, the desert had perils of its own. The forest had been humid, but the desert's dry, arid heat was far less bearable. Without trees providing cover the sun's rays beat down on them like a driving storm. The heat seemed to add weight to the pack on Sam's back as he trudged across the uneven terrain. He felt heat from the sand right through his shoes; he imagined the sand being as hot to the touch as a hunk of molten steel from the Foundry.

Thomas and Rand draped the old shirts Jack had stolen from the inn around their heads to keep the sun's rays off their faces. Joan was wearing the blouse like a shawl, her bushy hair flattened beneath it. There was enough sand in Sam's boots for him to start a desert of his own. He'd finished his first water gourd and was working on his second, but his mouth stayed stale and dry as ever.

By midday exhaustion began to take its steady hold, and their supply of water became critical. They turned to the fruits they packed hoping their juice would quench their thirst, but they were so warm they couldn't bring themselves to eat them. What little water that remained had become so warm it was like drinking a flavorless soup. Rand tried chilling the containers in his hands, but the heat returned in minutes.

"This is torture," Joan said, her face nearly as red as her hair. "How do these people live out here? It's worse out here than the magma chambers back home."

She stopped to catch her breath, letting her satchel fall to the sand behind her. She dug around inside the bag and growled when she found she'd drunk the last of her water. "Great, just great." She let the empty gourds tumble into the sand, kicking one out of sight in frustration.

"You should have rationed it like the rest of us," Rand said.

"Well, excuse me, but we can't all keep ourselves cool like you can."

"I am far from keeping cool," Rand pushed sweat slicked hair from his pink face. "I can only lower the temperature if there's moisture in the air. I'm just as overheated out here as any of you." He turned to Sam. "Shouldn't we have reached it by now?"

Sam flipped back and forth between two pages, squinting up at the sun. By his estimation they were heading due west like the book instructed, but there was no tower to be seen. As far as he could tell there wasn't so much as a boulder poking through the never-ending sands. "It has to be around here somewhere..."

"Maybe the *spirits* are hiding it from us," Joan wiggled her fingers in front of Sam's face. "Maybe we're not worthy after all? Oh, desert spirits?" she called, her voice loud and mocking. "A little help over here would be great right about now!"

"Don't do that," Sam said.

"Why not?"

"It's disrespectful, that's why not."

Joan snorted. "We're here to help, aren't we? If they are real they should be leading us straight there!" She turned away and faced the open dunes. "Hey! Dead guys! Where is this damn tower already?"

Sam cringed as her voice echoed across the dunes, the desert remaining quiet and empty as ever. The only sound that could be heard was the faint push of the breeze and their collective heavy breathing.

"Guess that answers that," Joan taunted Sam.

"That wasn't funny," Sam said.

"What's funny is you actually believe that nonsense," Joan shook her head and checked her pack again for a gourd she may have missed. "What a bunch of superstitious-"

"Look!"

Thomas pointed to the east, where a section of the desert was blurred by what looked like a distant cloud of dust. A hot breeze blew over them as the sand at their feet began to move. The cloud began to expand along the horizon, hiding the dunes in a twinkling haze.

Thomas looked uneasy. "Is that-?"

"A sandstorm," Sam finished, glaring at Joan. "Now you've done it."

"Come on, you think I did that?"

"You just couldn't keep your mouth shut, could you? You just had to make a joke of it!"

"Well if we could just find this stupid tower of yours it wouldn't be a problem, would it?"

"We wouldn't have a problem if you'd just kept your mouth shut!"

"Don't be an idiot, there's nothing out here but sand!"

"That's for sure," Thomas said, backing away in fear.

The cloud sped across the dunes at an alarming rate, the whipping grit hurtling in their direction like a tidal wave. With what little strength they had left they sprinted off, as the savage winds howled at their heels. Sam could feel the wind picking up on his back, nearly blowing his hat of his head. He grabbed it and stuffed it in the pocket of his coat, as furious cloud drew less than a few hundred yards away.

"We need to find the tower, now!" Sam shouted over the wailing winds, his fingers shielding his eyes from the dust.

"No kidding!" Joan screamed back.

"Just keep running west, we have to be close!"

"We can't outrun a sandstorm!" The short blew off Joan's head, her hair flying in all directions. "I knew this was a bad-"

Her last words turned to screams as the sand beneath her shifted and started pulling her down. Her brother dove toward her as she clawed at the ground but in moments she disappeared beneath the surface. Thomas began to frantically dig when he too began sinking, and was pulled under the sand with his sister. Before either Rand or Sam could even react they too began to slip, swallowed by the sands as the storm swept the desert.

# ABOUT THE AUTHOR

Kyle Viera was born in Massachusetts where he has lived his entire life. Growing up inspired by a love of stories, at twenty-two he began his dream of telling one of his own. *Strong* is his first published work after years of early mornings, sleepless nights, and countless cups of black coffee. He hopes to have Part Two available within a year, with another series well in the works.

Aside from writing and reading Kyle enjoys spending time with his son, the outdoors and playing music with friends.